Dragons Blood:
Odyssey to Dionysodoros

TALES FROM
THE MEN OF BRONZE

VINCENT PATRICK LEEPART

Tellwell Talent
www.tellwell.ca

ISBN
978-1-77370-951-2 (Paperback)
978-1-77370-952-9 (eBook)

To my wife Elaine:

Who put up with me coming home every night after work and writing until I couldn't see straight.

To my friend Devon:

Master of Dungeons
Slayer of Dragons

Dragon's Blood:

Odyssey to Dionysodoros

1

L oud banging on the door to his room at the inn woke Gamden from a drunken sleep. The night before he had celebrated with friends at the tavern on the main floor, spending his spoils from the latest venture that Dramen had sent him on. Again, there was a banging on the door, but this time a deep voice shouted: "Get your ass out of bed, Dramen is waiting for you!"

Gamden threw back the covers and shivered from the cold, then rubbed his eyes and slowly got up from the bed. The coal basket in the corner of the room had long since burnt out and the morning sun that was shining into his room had no warmth. His clothes littered the floor, along with the empty wine bottles that were evidence of how good of a time it had been. With blurry eyes, he tripped over one of the bottles and fell into a chair by the door.

More banging on the door, and the deep voice said: "I don't have time for this crap, open the door or I'll break it down and drag you to Dramen." Gamden reached for the door latch, unlocked it and opened it. Hoset stood in the doorway, glaring down at Gamden. His red hair, pale skin and blue eyes made him stand out in the three kingdoms, where everyone else had brown eyes and olive skin.

"You don't want to keep Dramen waiting, he is impatient today," Hoset said, with a warning in his voice, and he walked into the room, ducking to make the doorway. "Get dressed and make it fast, Gamden." Hoset made for an imposing figure. He stood well above any other man, and in his full leather armour he looked like a giant.

"I know, I know." said Gamden, with a smirk. "I celebrated with my mates and one very lucky barmaid last night. She left with a bag of copper coins and a sore cunny." Hoset shook his head, laid his hand on the pommel of his sword and growled "Get dressed now." Gamden rooted around for a leather strap to tie his shoulder-length hair back. He then looked up at Hoset and smiled, revealing a bright white smile and full lips. He had light brown eyes that hinted at something more but kept their secrets within, and an aquiline nose perfectly proportioned to his face. While getting dressed, he asked Hoset: "Don't you ever do anything fun? I mean, go to the taverns and have some wine or ale? Or maybe try to talk to a pretty girl?"

Hoset laughed and said, with scorn: "Dramen has many chores for me, so I have no spare time for such things."

"I believe you," replied Gamden, after a big swig from an open bottle of wine. "You don't know what you're missing, though." He smiled and finished off the bottle.

"I want for nothing!" asserted Hoset. "Dramen compensates me for all my hard work. The finest wine and women are offered to me for my choosing."

Gamden pulled on his boots and put on his jacket. "I'm ready to go, don't want to keep Dramen waiting." Hoset turned and ducked through the doorway, Gamden followed and closed the door behind them. "Let's stop for something to eat first, I'm so hungry I could eat a handful of eggs and the chicken that laid them."

Nothing but silence from Hoset as they walked down the dimly-lit narrow hallway.

"Come on, I'm serious, I'm really hungry!"

"No!" Grunted Hoset.

"Please?"

Without warning, Hoset stopped dead in his tracks and spun around to face Gamden, who wasn't paying attention and walked straight into his chest, then stumbled backward into the wall behind him.

In his most menacing voice, Hoset said, "Didn't you hear me, Dramen is impatient!" Hoset grabbed him by the scruff of the neck, lifting him off the ground with ease. "Don't make me impatient, too!"

"OK, OK! I'll wait till later!"

They exited the inn and walked the empty streets to the centre of the city. The air was cold. Clouds and black smoke from all the businesses and homes burning coal helped to conceal the sun. In the distance, King Arton's palace towered above all the other buildings in the city of Amenophis. "Hoset, do you know what Dramen wants from me this time?" panted Gamden, as he almost had to run to keep up with Hoset's long strides.

"No, I don't, but he said that if you didn't want to come willingly I was to tell you that he would make it worth your while to come see him. Make what you will of that."

"Last time, Dramen said that I almost got myself killed in a dungeon looking for his Gauntlet of Titan Strength."

"I really don't care." answered Hoset, as they approached the palace. They walked into the courtyard and made their way to the left of the main doors, where Dramen had a small library where he held meetings that the King shouldn't know about.

Hoset unlocked the door to the library, swinging it open to reveal Dramen sitting at a desk at the back of the room in his green dressing robe. Candelabra on either end of a table in the middle of the room revealed books new and old lining the shelves behind him, while chalkboards full of runes and ancient alphabets lined the other walls. Concentrating on the scroll in front of him, he said without looking up: "You finally chose to grant me your audience. My time is important these days. So much research for your next job."

Gamden walked across the room to the desk and asked, "Where are you sending me this time, and how much gold will I get?"

Dramen sat back to reveal a face weathered by age, but containing piercing grey eyes that looked right into a man's soul.

"Straight to business this morning, then. Fine, you will get no gold," said Dramen.

"I don't work for free." Gamden spun around and was ready to walk out when he heard: "You will get no gold, Gamden. No, you will get this small chest of diamonds." Dramen wrapped a fur cloak over his shoulders, got up from his chair and walked to the table in the middle of the room. There he opened a small chest full of perfectly cut diamonds.

Gamden looked over his shoulder and said: "Diamonds? I like your terms so far, but you still haven't told me where I'm going. Must be pretty bad if you're offering me diamonds."

"If you get me what I need, Gamden, you can have so much more. You're going to get me dragon's blood!"

"I can't kill a dragon!" Gamden threw his arms in the air as he walked toward Dramen. "You're crazy! Keep your diamonds and I'll keep my life!"

"No, No. You misunderstand me, Gamden. You will be killing no dragon. You will be going to a dragon nest…"

"But?" said Gamden.

"But you will be going to the ancient keep of Azerta," Continued Dramen. "That's why I am offering a king's ransom of diamonds. I agree it is a formidable task, but it is one that I know you can accomplish for me."

"This sounds far too easy," said Gamden, with a distrusting look on his face.

"You're absolutely right," answered Dramen. "The danger is not at the dragon's nest. The danger waits for you at the keep. The latest reports from my scouts tell me that the eastern Khans are throwing their weight behind the cyclops monarch, Brontes. They want to take back Dionysodoros and control the Neferkare sea trade, starving out the three kingdoms." Dramen walked around the table and put his hand on Gamden's shoulder, and said, "You have never failed me before, and you won't this time, either."

"I appreciate the vote of confidence, Dramen."

"Now, come look at this map, Gamden, and make a drawing for yourself." Dramen gestured to the scroll rolled out on the table, then explained the safest route for the trip to Azerta as Gamden quickly copied it. "My scouts also tell me that hundreds of mercenaries from the Eastern Khans have taken over the villages surrounding Azerta."

"Wait!" blurted out Gamden. "You mean that I have to make my way through an army of mercenaries, too?"

"You'll be fine, boy, no problem for you."

Gamden went visibly pale. "This just keeps getting better, doesn't it!?"

From the corner of the room, Hoset's laugh was dripping with ridicule toward Gamden.

"Shut up, Hoset!" countered Gamden.

Hoset menacingly took a step forward, but Dramen waved him off and he backed away reluctantly.

"I still don't understand how I am going to get this dragon blood," said Gamden. "How do I do that without killing a dragon?"

"That is why I asked you here on the winter solstice," replied Dramen. "Dragons give birth once every ten years, and this is the year. By the time you get there, the juvenile dragon will be able to leave the nest and you can collect the blood from the afterbirth."

"The blood will be dried and useless, won't it?" asked Gamden. "What good is dry blood to you?"

"Only those who can read the ancient texts, which I can," asserted Dramen, "know that dragon's blood is liquid until the dragon is dead. So, even the blood in the afterbirth will be useful, as long as the newborn dragon lives."

"Why does Brontes allow the dragons to nest at Azerta? queried Gamden. "He could remove them if he wanted to, couldn't he?"

"Brontes, being a cyclops, was created by the gods." responded Dramen. "Dragons were also created by the gods and are much more powerful than he. He has no choice in the matter."

Gamden thought about the task before him for a moment, and then said: "You have a deal, Dramen, but I need another thousand gold pieces to hire some mercenaries of my own to help with this one, and mercenaries deal in gold, not diamonds."

"Done," said Dramen. "Take what you need. Just get my dragon's blood!"

"Hoset!" shouted Dramen. "Get my little thief friend here as much gold as he wants from my purse, and then show him the door out!"

2

Gamden collected his swag and left the library full of worry and doubt. Lost in his own world, he walked aimlessly through the streets of the city toward the inn and thought to himself: *Dramen thinks I don't know how dangerous this job is. Sea voyages are just the beginning. I hate ships! I bet the city guard at Khaemwaset hasn't forgotten about how I made them look like fools when I made off with the King's prized bottle of wine. What made things worse was when I broke into the Captain of the Guard's room later that night and left the empty bottle on his pillow. Now that I look back, I probably shouldn't have done it. If they spot me when I go looking for Senusret, I'll be rotting in the stockade till I'm old and feeble. When I get to Azerta, the eastern wildmen won't be a problem, they will be easily amazed and frightened by my magic. The cyclops monarch will be hard to get past. Cyclopes are smart and very mean, known to pull intruders limb from limb.*

When Gamden finally reached the inn, he went to the pub and sat down at a table. The barkeep walked over and said,

"Why so glum?" as he dried his hands on his soiled apron. "Last night you were having such a good time."

"I took on a new job today and it's going to be a tough one." answered Gamden. "Might have bitten off more than I can chew."

"Sounds dangerous. Maybe you should pay your tab from last night and sleep with a clear conscience tonight," he said, with a smile on his face.

"Maybe you're right," said Gamden, with a laugh. Reaching into his breast pocket he pulled out a diamond and pressed it into the sweaty palm of the barkeep.

The barkeep whistled in amazement. "This is far more than what you owe me."

"Like you said, leave with a clear conscience. And maybe that will get me a couple of bottles of wine for tonight, too!"

The next morning, Gamden woke and started his day early. His bedroll and haversack over his shoulder, he went to the market and bought what he needed for the trip to Khaemwaset to find his old traveling mate. He could trust him with his life, and the last time they were together there was no bad blood. Gamden made his way through the narrow streets of the city, down to the farmlands that sprawled before him and led to the cliffs. The weather was cool and a light snow was falling, covering the hearty winter crops. The roads were now wet and coated his boots in slick mud that was going to make the descent to the docks treacherous. Falling more times than he could remember, Gamden made it to the harbor, where he looked for a seaworthy ship with a captain he could trust. As evening came with cloudy skies, the sun disappeared and the snow that was falling up at city level had turned to rain at sea level. He talked to many captains, and nearly all of them were too drunk to stand. One skipper was loading his cockboat with supplies to take to his ship anchored off in the distance. He was coming back one more time for the last of his cargo, then was departing for Khaemwaset.

After waiting a while, Gamden made his way back to where the cockboat should have been, but only empty water greeted him. "Damn it!" he shouted, and kicked at a gull that flew away squawking. A voice shouted back to him out of the mist that concealed the end of the dock. "Hey, you still need passage to Khaemwaset?"

"Yeah, I'll pay you whatever you want!" Gamden shouted back.

"Get yer ass down here! The last of me cargo is loaded and we're ready to weigh anchor as soon as we get back to the ship!"

Gamden ran to the end of the dock, where the boat, four men and the skipper waited impatiently. As Gamden approached, a single lantern at the bow dimly lit the area. All of them wore long coats to keep out the cold, damp sea air. The skipper's long black hair was oily and fell over his shoulders. A scar ran across his face, starting above his right eye and running down to his left upper lip.

"Ten gold pieces will get ya across the Chepren Sea. My ship is small and has no creature comforts, and ya will have to sleep in the cargo hold. Ya don't like me terms then ya can swim," snarled the skipper.

Gamden's stomach was already turning from the thought of the sea voyage. "Ten gold pieces sounds good to me."

As he reached into his pocket for the gold, the skipper said, "I run a dry ship, lad, no booze. If I catch ya with a drink in ya hand I'll have ya thrown off the ship."

Gamden looked at the size of the four men near the captain, swallowed audibly and said in a meek voice: "Sounds good to me," then handed over the gold coins.

"All right, lads," commanded the skipper. "Get in the cockboat and let's make for the ship." The skipper sat at the bow and the four crewmen manned the oars, while Gamden searched in vain for a comfortable place to sit. It only took a couple of minutes to get to the ship. Lanterns at the bow and stern dimly lit the rickety old vessel in the mist.

"Oh, shit," Gamden said out loud, by mistake.

The skipper heard him and said in gruff manner: "What'sa matter lad, ya don't like the look of me ship? She may be old, but she sails the seas like no one's business. Ain't that right, lads?"

"Aye, skipper," all four crewmen said, in unison.

"No slaver, no warship can keep up with her," continued the skipper.

"Haven't kept all me fingers this long by being the slowest ship."

"How did you get the scar on your face?" asked Gamden.

The skipper reached up without thinking and touched the scar. He looked off into the mist for a moment, lost in his memories.

"Skipper, are you all right?" asked Gamden.

He shook his head, loosening the cobwebs that memories spin.

"Huh? What ya say, lad? Oh yes, me scar. Been a long time since anyone asked about me scar."

The cockboat came alongside the ship, ropes were lowered and the oars stowed. The lowered ropes were secured into the rowlocks and the pulleys on the ship squealed to life under the weight.

The skipper continued by saying, "Got this scar from me first captain, disobeyed a direct order, got the business end of a whip across me face. Cut me good." The skipper reached into his coat and presented a whip. "This whip here, as a matter of fact."

"Did your captain give you that whip?" asked Gamden.

"No lad, I killed him and took the whip, then took his ship. This ship here, as a matter of fact." The skipper made a sweeping gesture with his arm. "How d'ya like that, lad?" The skipper slapped Gamden hard on the shoulder, laughed and walked away, saying: "Ask one of me men to show you where to sleep. Hope ya brought yer own food, I ain't feedin' ya!"

The skipper left Gamden standing amongst the crewmen, who were busy storing cargo and getting the ship ready to sail. One of the crewmen walked up behind him and said, "Don't worry about it, kid." Startled, Gamden spun around and found himself face to face with an old man. His long coat was torn and patched in many places. His head was shaved, revealing several liver spots, and his long grey beard was braided and hung down almost to his belt. "Skipper is an asshole, everyone knows that and so does he. Now you do, too." Gamden let out a nervous laugh. The old man continued, "I'll make sure that you're comfortable below decks and get you some hot soup after we're underway."

Gamden held out his hand and said, "Thanks for that, my name is Gamden."

The old man took his hand and replied, "You're welcome, kid. My name is Achaemenes. Always a treat to find a new friend, and someone different to talk to than these bounders." Gamden finally started to feel at ease in this unfamiliar place. They made their way below decks through the maze of cargo, livestock and crewmen. Somewhere near midships, Achaemenes stopped and said, "Here are some nice, dry sacks of grain to sleep on for the trip." Achaemenes hung his lantern on a thick wooden beam and said, "I'll leave this lantern here for you, just remember to snuff it before you fall asleep."

"How will you make it to the deck? It's pitch black outside this room," asked Gamden.

"Don't worry about it, kid. I know every part of this ship by heart. I'll be back in a little bit with that soup I promised you."

Achaemenes left the room and Gamden said to himself, "Might as well get out of these cold, wet clothes." As he struggled to get his boots off, he heard the skipper shout the order for full sail. Pulleys began to squeal, ropes and beams groaned under the weight of the main sail going up the mast. The wind caught hold of the sail and the ship lurched forward, almost throwing Gamden off the sacks of grain.

The sea was always rough in winter and this year was no different. Gamden could feel when the ship left the breakwater and headed out to the open sea. For the first couple of minutes the water in the harbour was calm, but past the breakwater the waves of the Chephren Sea began to smash into the bow of the ship. Just as old Achaemenes promised, he returned with a full bowl of soup. He caught sight of Gamden's pale face and said, "You look terrible, kid, eat this soup and you will feel better. My own special recipe. I add the thisimus root, settles the stomach. Been doing it for years."

Gamden thanked him and took the bowl, then added, "I've never liked to travel by sea, my stomach always does somersaults. Plus, I'm terrified of ships. The thought of drowning is horrible." Gamden rambled on, nervously.

Achaemenes laughed out loud, and said, "Don't worry kid, this old ship will never sink." He touched the beam above his head with affection. "Now, eat the soup and you'll feel better. Skipper says we have a strong wind in the sail and will be in Nebetah in a couple days."

The voyage was boring for Gamden. The weather was cold and wet, so he stayed below deck and studied the map that he had copied from Dramen's library and caught up on his sleep. Gamden knew that they had arrived at the port city of Nebetah when the ship came to a jarring halt and the anchor was lowered onto the seafloor. He got dressed quickly, his clothes were still a little damp but better than before. He scraped the flint in the lantern together and lit the wick, and made his way to the deck. Just as he was reaching for the cargo door, it flew open revealing old Achaemenes's smiling face. A gust of cold sea air met his nostrils and he inhaled deeply, smiling back.

"Nothing smells better after a couple nights in the cargo hold, hey kid?"

"You got that right!" answered Gamden. "Smells like home!"

Once on deck, he saw that darkness and stars were still in the morning sky. In the distance a lighthouse flickered, revealing other ships in the harbour.

"You got family here, kid?" asked Achaemenes, as they walked across the deck to where the cockboat was being prepared to go to shore.

"No, I'm going to find an old friend in Khaemwaset. Should be holed up in one of the pubs there." Gamden placed a hand on the headrail and continued, "He loves his drink, so that should be the best place to start."

From the stern of the ship, the skipper could be heard shouting orders about what he wanted loaded into the cockboat for the first trip to shore. Making his way to the bow, he kept on shouting at the crew to get things done faster, and when he came up to Gamden, he said, "And I suppose ya will want to go to shore right away too, won't ya?"

"Y...yes," stammered Gamden. "Yes, I would love to get to shore, Skipper."

The skipper spun around and shouted, "Take those sacks of grain out! The lad wants to go ashore with me!"

"Aww, c'mon skipper! Just got 'em in!" groaned one of the crewmen.

"Shut up and do as yer told!" shouted the skipper as he stormed off.

Gamden turned back to Achaemenes and said, "I have something special for you." Reaching into his pack, he pulled out a handful of dates and gave them to his new friend.

Immediately, his face lit up with a smile and he thanked Gamden.

"Oooh, I love dates! This really is a treat, I can never afford them. Thank you so much."

From the cockboat, the skipper shouted, "Git yer ass over here lad, or I'll leave ya here to rot!"

Gamden ran to the boat and jumped in. He waved one last time to Achaemenes.

3

Gamden wasn't sure if it was a good idea to go into Khaemwaset. The city guard would most certainly remember what he did the last time he was in town. Good thing he knew the kind of people that live their lives in the shadows. He will have to slip some gold coins into the hands of a few old friends to get in the front gates. First stop will be the Crown & Jester tavern to talk to Jardz, he knows everything that goes on in Khaemwaset, and everyone. Nebetah was an old city, built around a natural harbour in the southern part of the island. The inner city was basically a shantytown, while the gentry had their palaces and mansions on the outskirts. Making his way through streets crowded with vendors and thieves, he arrived at the tavern. Gamden walked into a noisy room full of people drinking and eating. He walked up to the bar, found an empty mug and banged it loudly to attract the attention of the tapster. Quickly, a tall young man with boring brown eyes and dark clothes walked over and said, "What's your poison?"

"I'll have an ale," replied Gamden.

"Copper piece up front," said the barkeep. "No tabs."

The barkeep tapped his fingers impatiently while Gamden fished through his pockets. His pouch had nothing but gold and diamonds and Gamden didn't want that kind of wealth displayed openly in this place.

Finding the correct pocket, he pulled out a handful of copper pieces, buttons and coloured pebbles, spilled them out on the counter and found a coin. The barkeep grunted, scooped up the tender and went to get some ale. Gamden looked around, trying to find Jardz in the room, but no luck. When the tapster returned, Gamden asked him, "Where's Jardz? Can't see him."

"Who wants to know?" asked the barkeep.

"Me? Oh, I'm no one special. I just need to ask Jardz a couple questions."

"If you need to know it will cost you," the barkeep looked down and pointed to the buttons and pebbles. "Looks like you can't afford nothin'," then laughed in Gamden's face.

"Would this be enough?" Gamden pulled out a nice, bright, gold coin stamped with the crowns of the three kingdoms from the pouch hanging around his neck.

The bartender whistled, then said, "How did you get the King's gold?" Three drunks next to Gamden overheard the conversation and stumbled toward them.

"What's this about the King's gold?"

"Shut up, ya drunken fools, and go away!" said the barkeep in a menacing tone. "Or I'll have ya thrown out on yer asses!"

"No, you shut up, and this young'un here can share some of that gold!" one of the drunks said while wringing his hands.

"Ahmose! Get over here, now!" called out the barkeep.

From the other end of the bar came a tall, fat, young man in thick black leather pants, boots and studded vest. The drunks never saw him coming. Ahmose backhanded one of them so hard that he flew several feet through the air, crashing unconscious into the nearby table. The other two turned around in time to feel him smash their heads together, and they, too, fell to the ground unconscious. "They owe you money, boss?"

"Nah, they're just pissin' me off." The barkeep thought about what should be done with them, then continued, "Throw them in the gutter to sleep it off."

"OK, boss." Ahmose grabbed the two drunks at his feet by their collars with one hand, then walked over and grabbed the third drunk with the other and dragged them away.

Gamden sighed a breath of relief that no one else heard what just happened. He had to keep a low profile while he was here, especially with all the gold and diamonds in his pouch.

"You a bounty hunter on the King's business?" asked the bartender.

"No, I'm on my way to Khaemwaset, and I need to find a friend."

The barkeep looked him up and down, then said, "Well, you look too young to be of any danger." He pointed to the balcony, then continued, "He's in his private room in the back, high-stakes bare-knuckle fight. Jardz has a lot of gold riding on his man. When you get up there, tell the doorman I said it was OK."

Gamden grabbed his ale and made his way through the crowd to the staircase. Every stair seemed to have a drunk or a prostitute on it trying to get coin anyway they could. When he made it to the top of the stairs, he quickly went through all his pockets to make sure that nothing was missing. Sure that he had not been pickpocketed, he walked up to the doorman and said, "The bartender said that I could get in to see Jardz."

The doorman, who was dressed like the minder downstairs, looked down and across the room to the bartender, who nodded his head and gave thumbs up. The doorman was satisfied with that, he unlocked the door and allowed Gamden to pass. Gamden walked into a small arena where two men were fighting. Torches lined the wall. Beaten and polished silver mirrors behind each torch lit the room perfectly. Jardz sat at one end of the oval in a chair that was raised above the action, while his opponent sat across from him in a similarly raised position. Several other people surrounded the arena, cheering and betting on the combatants. Gamden walked up to where Jardz sat and shouted,

"Jardz! Jardz, it's Gamden!" No luck, he was completely involved with the match. Gamden jumped up and down and waved his arms, and shouted out again, but to no avail.

Jardz was a big fat man who ate and drank ale all day but could crush your skull between his hands, and he was known to do so to those who crossed him. He dressed in a toga for convenience. Being so fat, he didn't bother with pants and such.

Knowing that it was a waste of time trying to get Jardz' attention anymore, Gamden made his way to the fight and watched for a bit, but also kept an eye on Jardz. Two men near the boards of the arena were betting on the fight.

"Twenty gold coins that Adelphius' man will take the fight in the next two minutes!"

"I'll take that bet!" the other man shouted back.

The fighters exchanged several blows, then Jardz' fighter knocked his opponent to the ground. Jardz stood up and shouted over everyone else, "He's down! Finish him! Finish him now!"

In the blink of an eye, the fighter mounted his rival. Three blows to the jaw and an elbow to the temple and the match was over.

"Yes!" shouted Jardz. "Yes! I win again!" He climbed down from his chair and waddled across the room to his opponent, laughing all the way. No matter where you were in a room you could hear Jardz over everything else: "It was a good fight, but my boy has never lost." He grabbed his sack of gold, turned around and, with an enormous smile on his face, shouted, "Drinks are on me tonight!"

Everyone in the room cheered their appreciation.

Jardz paid his fighter the gold pieces he had promised him, then waddled toward the balcony overlooking the tavern. Gamden saw his chance, ran up to Jardz while he was still in a good mood and said, "Jardz, hey Jardz. It's me, Gamden. Do you have a couple minutes for me?"

"What? Who? Oh, Gamden, my boy. Yes! Come drink with me and celebrate my victory!" shouted Jardz, as he gave Gamden a hearty slap on the back that knocked the wind right out of him. For a big fat man, Jardz toddled along quickly and Gamden had to double-time it to keep up. "Come on boy, I'm thirsty! Let's get some ale in us!" He burst through the doors to the balcony and shouted, "Get me and my friend some ale, now!" Jardz kept a tapster and wench upstairs for just such occasions. Completely out of breath, Jardz collapsed into his chair. The doorman walked over and took the sack of gold. Jardz held on to it for a second, reached into the bag and took out two gold pieces. "This is for you, boy. Put my winnings with the rest, then come back and get some ale for yourself."

Gamden was served a stein of ale and Jardz received two tankards overflowing with ale by the wench. "Drink with me, m'boy!" shouted Jardz. They toasted one another, Gamden had a couple of quick drinks while Jardz emptied his tankard in one big swig. As he did, some ale spilled down the many rolls of his neck, soaking his toga down the front. When he had emptied his vessel, Jardz slammed it down on the table and stopped breathing for a moment, then belched loud and long. After wiping his mouth with the back of his hand, Jardz said, "What did you need to talk to me about?"

"Yeah, I need to find Senusret. Have you seen him lately?"

"Senusret, of course I have" Jardz paused to have another drink of ale, then continued. "He just finished a job for me. Should be in Khaemwaset right now, that's where he said he was going. Had some debts to take care of. He's a good boy! I hire him when I need someone to collect on debts. Ha! Funny, isn't it. The boy had to collect on my debts to pay his!" Jardz laughed heartily at his own joke.

"Perfect, I know exactly where he should be, then. One more thing, Jardz, I'm going to need some help getting back into Khaemwaset. You must know some people that can help me get past the guard."

Jardz wiped the sweat away from his forehead, laughed, then said, "Yes, I remember now. You made the Captain of the Guard look the fool, and because of that I'm going to help you!" Jardz slapped Gamden on the shoulder so hard he fell out of his chair. "Me and the captain have conflicting ideas as to who supplies his city with alcohol and drugs." With that he drank the last of the ale in his tankard.

"Ah, that's great, Jardz." said Gamden, as he slowly got back into his chair.

"But first, let's drink, boy! Celebrate my victory! Wench, bring me and my friend here more ale!" shouted Jardz.

4

Vague memories came back to Gamden as he slowly opened his eyes. Drinking heavily was the first one to emerge, then the wench half-undressed on his lap. Finally, Jardz was carrying him like a rag doll in his massive arms... to where? The room was unfamiliar but felt safe, and he was clothed as well. An audible sigh of relief came out of Gamden as he closed his hand on the pouch of gold and diamonds around his neck. Stumbling through the darkness, he found a door and opened it to reveal a room well-lit by candles from a chandelier in the middle of the room. Klinai were against all four walls. The largest one held Jardz sitting upright, sleeping naked women on either side of him. The other klinai contained Jardz' bodyguards, all sleeping except for one who was nursing a mug of ale and talking to a prostitute. Gamden made his way over and asked the bodyguard, "How long was I out for?"

"Not sure," answered the bodyguard. "I got here when the water clock was refilled, and it's empty now so it should be sunrise soon."

"Perfect," sighed Gamden. "I still have time to make it to the rendezvous point to meet the smugglers." He looked around quickly for paper and something to write with. By the door he found a desk with a quill pen, jotted down a quick note and handed it to the bodyguard. "Make sure Jardz gets this, please. I owe him one."

"I can do that for ya! Must be a good friend of Jardz'. Never seen him take care of a person like he did you."

"What do you mean?" asked Gamden.

"Jardz gave all of us strict instructions to make sure nothing happened to you."

"Wow, must have really impressed him by making enemies with the Captain of the Guard," Gamden said to himself, then he thanked the bodyguard again and high-tailed it for the street.

Running through the streets of Nebetah in the early dawn light, Gamden had to fight his way through the vendors setting up shop. Carts blocked his progress at every turn. He had to meet the smugglers this morning or he would lose his chance to get into the city. Even worse, Jardz wouldn't give him another chance like this ever again. Finally, he reached the stables where he had to ask for Nergal. Jardz said to mention his name and safe passage would be granted. Once inside the stables, he found a boy and asked him where to find Nergal.

"You can find him over there." The boy pointed to an old man standing near a horse-drawn cart being filled with sacks of grain.

Gamden thanked the boy and ran off to find his contact. Completely out of breath, Gamden said to the old man, "Are you Nergal?"

"Aye, that I am. What can I do fer ya?"

"Jardz told me to meet you here to get me into the city without any trouble from the guard."

"Then ye must be Gamden."

"Yeah, how do you know? asked Gamden, with a puzzled look on his face.

"He sent one of his men to see me last night, interrupted me supper. Pissed about that, I was! Told me to expect a young lad named Gamden in the morning and to get 'im into the city nice and quiet like." The last sack of grain was loaded into the cart.

"We're ready to go, lad." Nergal reached into his long black coat and pulled a cap from the inside pocket. "Hope you brought something to keep yer head warm. Wind is strong today, gonna be cold on the road to Khaemwaset." With years of practice, Nergal climbed up into the driver's seat of the cart, held out his hand and continued, "Take my hand, lad, no footsteps on that side of the cart. Never needed 'em, just me every day, all day, up and down the hill."

Gamden took his hand, climbed up the spokes of the wheel and took the seat next to him. A snap of the reins and the horses dug their hooves into the soil, jerking the cart forward. "You're right," said Gamden. "It's going to be a cold ride." Rummaging through his haversack, Gamden pulled out a thick scarf and wrapped it around his neck and face. With the scarf muffling his voice and the wind wiping the words right out of his mouth, Gamden shouted, "Thank you for getting me into the city!"

"That's all right, lad. When Jardz asks you to do something for him...well, let's just say that it would be a mistake to say no."

"How do you know Jardz?" asked Gamden.

"The two of us were fighters."

"You mean that you were both gladiators?"

"No Lad, Jardz and me fought with our fists and feets, no weapons."

"I never knew that Jardz was a fighter." Right after he said it, Gamden thought back to last night when he was in the arena and it all made sense.

"We never fought each other and I'm glad fer that, I tell ya. Jardz never lost a fight. Killed three men in the arena he did, by accident, of course. He's just too strong!"

"So, you're doing this for Jardz because you two are such good friends?" asked Gamden.

"No lad, I'm doing this because he saved me life. I was fighting earlier in the night one time and Jardz was the main attraction. The fighter I was up against somehow got a small blade into the arena. Took out me eye he did, and Jardz saw what he done. Jumped in the ring and snapped his neck like a twig, Jardz did." Nergal turned to look at Gamden and continued, "Got me this eye he did, to replace the one that bastard cut out of me head." He tapped it with his finger. Gamden looked closer and noticed a perfectly white quartz eyeball in the socket, with a jade iris and an obsidian pupil. He shivered with the thought of the pain Nergal went through.

For the rest of the trip along the cargo trail, Gamden listened to Nergal talk all the way up. What was worse was that it started to get colder and snow started blowing the further they climbed up the trail.

Just before the crest of the hill the cart came to a stop, and Nergal said, "Now lad, get in the back and move a few of them sacks, lay down and cover yerself with 'em." Once Gamden was covered, the cart lurched forward. Gamden struggled to get comfortable under the sacks, then made a gap to see out of. Nergal whistled a traveling tune as they continued toward Khaemwaset. First, Gamden saw the small villages that surrounded the King's city, followed by the farms and the stables that fed it. Everyone is prosperous here, and loyal to the King. Finally, they reached the parapet where armed guards wrapped in heavy fur coats and hats kept watch. One of them stepped forward, faced the cart and shouted out, "Stop where you are! Make yourself known!"

"It's me Igmilum, it's always me, right on time as usual. Gotta get the grain to the miller or he'll have me head on a pike."

"Yes, yes Nergal. I know it's you, but if I don't follow orders the officer on watch will have *my* head on a pike." The guard jerked his thumb over his shoulder at the officer sitting near the fire, nice and warm.

Nergal and the guard laughed out loud at the joke, the same joke they laugh over at the same time every day. "Get going then, off to the miller. When you come back through I'll be finished my watch, and we'll have a quick drink." The guard pulled a silver flask from his fur coat, enticing Nergal.

With a big smile on his face, Nergal said, "Aye, that will warm me bones for the road home." With a snap of the reins, the horses snorted and the cart heaved toward the gates. Whistling away as the cart went through the main gates into Khaemwaset, Nergal said, "Stay in the cart, lad, till we get to the miller. There ye can be on yer way. Guards don't patrol around there, too far from the barracks." Nergal laughed out loud while he continued, "Lazy bastards!"

Gamden remained warm and out of the wind under the sacks. He watched as they went through the deserted city streets. Most of the merchant shops were closed because of the cold and the snow. Gamden recognized where they were at last and knew that it wouldn't be long until they were at their destination. The cart came to a stop outside a large stone building, and Nergal said, "We're here lad. Ye can be on yer way now."

Gamden crawled out from under the sacks into the cold wind and shivered. "Thanks for getting me into the city."

"Delivered ye safe and sound, I did," Nergal said, with a quick salute.

"Here, take this." Gamden reached into the pouch around his neck, pulled out a small diamond and pressed it into Nergal's palm.

"That's far too much, lad. I can't take this."

"A token of my appreciation and a down payment for the future. Never know when I'll need a friend in the city." Gamden returned the salute, turned and walked off down the snowy street.

"Made a friend of me ye did...a friend indeed!" shouted Nergal.

It was a long time ago that Gamden was last in the city, and he was sure that he knew where his mate would be. The first stop was at the Wild Hog tavern, still the best watering hole in all the castle walls. He had a long way to go, the miller was on the far side of the city and the tavern was in the centre. Halfway through the trek, the clouds broke, and the blowing snow stopped. The sun was warm, and he could take the scarf from around his neck and head. Gamden breathed deeply and enjoyed the warmth of the sun's rays on his face. Scooping snow into his hand, he ate until his stomach was full. After that long ride in the back of the cart he was thirsty. With the sun now shining, people came out of their homes and continued their day, and the closer he got to the centre of the city, the more people he came across. Gamden turned the last corner and there was the Wild Hog tavern. The doors were never locked, and people were constantly coming and going. The roar of the party inside could be heard clear across the lane. Making his way through the crowd at the front of the building, he got in the doors and right away the smell of ale and the unwashed mass of people made him cringe. Every table was full, and the floor was packed with partygoers. After what seemed forever, and several pickpocket attempts, Gamden made it to the bar. It was a long time since he had been in the tavern and he didn't recognize anybody. On a hunch, he went to the far end where the head mistress kept a seat for business. Qadira was there, as always, surrounded by her girls and enticing men and the odd woman with ease. Gamden walked up to her, she recognized him and said, "Hello handsome, haven't seen you in these parts for quite some time." When she spoke, she smiled and her face lit up like a diamond in sunlight. She was older than Gamden but still the most beautiful woman in all the three kingdoms. Her perfect brown eyes drew men to her like a thief to gold. Long black hair in ringlets draped over one shoulder. Her gown pushed up her breasts perfectly.

Blushing, Gamden took her hand in his and said, "Qadira, how do you become more beautiful every time I see you?" He flashed her a big smile.

Qadira gave him a sideways glance and replied, "You are so full of crap, but I appreciate the compliment." She got up and held her arms out for a hug. Taking him into her arms she pushed his head deep between her bosoms. "You're so damn handsome!" Lifting his head from between her bust, she kissed him passionately on the lips. Licking her lips as she drew away, she said in the most alluring voice, "If you keep up the sweet talk I might take you to my chamber, my treat." Cupping his genitals in her hand, she felt his erection and continued, "You know you want me!"

His eyes were still closed from the kiss. "Qadira…you tempt me like no other woman can, but I'm here on business." She punched him on the arm, breaking him from the trance. Sitting down, a look of complete rejection came over her face.

Immediately, Gamden got down on his knees before her and begged, "Please let me make it up to you!" He pulled out a gold coin from his pouch and pressed it to his lips. "Here take this!" He gently placed the coin in her palm. "Let me buy your drinks for the rest of the night."

Qadir saw the three crowns on the coin and a gasp escaped her lips. "The King's gold," she whispered. "You are here on business." She smiled again and continued, "I can't be mad at you!" She kissed him on the cheek. "At least have a glass of wine before you leave me brokenhearted."

One glass of wine turned into three. Entranced, Gamden just stared into her eyes and listened to her talk. Time had no meaning when in her presence and Gamden was in danger of being a slave to her love. Three men at the next table began fighting and tumbled over toward Gamden knocking him out of his chair. The trance broken, he came back to his senses. Two large bodyguards rushed in and scooped up the drunks, giving them a good beating as they threw them out the front door. Gamden finally remembered why he had come to see Qadir, and asked her, "Have you seen Senusret? Where can I find him?"

"What do you want with that brute? He's nothing but trouble," Qadir chided him and wagged her finger in his direction. She stopped mid-sentence, composed herself and then said, "You can find him sitting in the back, passed out as usual from too much wine and ale." She got up stepped toward Gamden, stroked his cheek lovingly and continued, "Be careful when you're around him."

"Don't worry about me. I always come out lookin' pretty." Gamden flashed her a big smile, turned and walked away quickly. Navigating through the crowd to the back of the tavern, he found Senusret without a problem. Following the loud snoring from the corner, he found him sleeping in his chair. Gamden shouted, and shook Senusret several times, but he wouldn't wake up. Looking around, he saw a pitcher full of water on the table next to him. Gamden threw the water in his face. Coughing and sputtering, Senusret bolted out of his seat and roared at the top of his lungs, "What'ya do that for! I was grabbing a quick snooze before the party starts again!" It took a second, but Senusret finally recognized him. "Gamden, aren't you a sight for sore eyes!" He bent down and scooped him up in his massive arms. *Woosh* went the air from his lungs as he was squeezed in a crushing bear hug.

"Put me down, put me down. You big bastard," squeaked Gamden.

"Sorry, I forget my own strength." Senusret dropped him to the floor. "Good to see you, it has been a long time since you were in Khaemwaset. Wait…why are you here in the city again? How did you get past the gate watch? You were run out of the city by the King's guard, no less. No easy task getting back in the city, I bet. That was great, every thief knew you're name. I'm so excited to see you I can't shut up!"

"First off, it's good to see you, too, and yes, I am taking a big risk coming back here, but it's worth it." Gamden took a quick look around to make sure that no one could overhear what he was going to say, especially one of the King's stool pigeons. "I'm going to make you rich, old friend. Rich enough to drown in wine and women."

"I like what you are saying so far, Gamden," he said with a grin from ear to ear. "You know me too well, but I also know that something that sounds that good is never that easy, old friend."

"You're right, Senusret, it isn't going to be that easy. I'm going to Azerta." Senusret was speechless for a change. "If you come with me you can line your pockets with three hundred gold coins, and five perfect diamonds."

Senusret found his voice. "I'm interested again, but that is a long trip, and very, very dangerous…"

"OK, OK. five hundred gold and five diamonds."

"That's better. I got lots of people that are wanting money out of me. If I don't die on the way there or back I better come home with more than enough."

"Good!" said Gamden. "Now that is settled, where is Khensu? We are going to need a skilled archer on the road."

"Khensu went to the Henuttawy monastery to become a priest. Haven't seen him in at least a year now."

"Seriously?" said Gamden, with a confused look on his face. "I never would have figured Khensu for a religious person. He loved to drink, swear and steal even more than you!" They both laughed about that. Drying the tears of laughter from his eyes, Gamden continued, "Henuttawy monastery is too far away for us to remain on schedule. I guess it's just us, then."

"You and me, Gamden, all the way. No one can stop us." Sensuret pounded his fist against his thick black leather breast armour, then shouted, "Unstoppable!" Senusret stood up again, and when he did he was almost double Gamden's height. Dark skin with close-cropped dark hair and beard, he was the perfect specimen of a southern warrior. Big dark eyes gave a look of inner strength and courage when he was set on a goal. Several scars and a flattened nose gave testament to a hard life on the streets. "Let's drink to our new partnership! I'm a little short on coin, though, you'll have to buy." Senusret pushed him toward the bar and was quick on his heels.

"I don't know if I should have drinks tonight. I was with Jardz last night and I can't remember too much."

"You were with Jardz? Lucky swine!" shouted Senusret, with a big smile. "Every time I do a job for him I get soooo drunk at his place, but he always makes me buy my own drinks."

The bartender walked up and asked, "What ya drinkin'?"

"Three flagons of your best wine!" shouted Senusret. "What do you want to drink, Gamden?"

Gamden looked up at Senusret, then over to the bartender and said, "Get this big bastard his flagons but make it cheap wine."

"Awww," said Senusret, through a frown.

"I'll have one for myself."

"Atta boy!" shouted Senusret, and smacked him on the back.

"Get right back in the bottle, I say!"

5

Gamden woke in a dimly lit room. A single oil lamp burned on the table in the corner. He couldn't remember how he got there and his head hurt from the cheap wine. "Never again," he muttered to himself as he slowly sat up. The next thought that came to him was where his pouch of gold and diamonds was. He felt for it around his neck, it wasn't there. Waves of nausea mixed with nervous anxiety caused him to break into a cold sweat. He got out of bed and staggered to where his clothes lay in a pile on the floor. Going through his coat pockets, pants pockets and shirt pockets, he found nothing. He couldn't go back to Dramen and ask for more gold. He would look the fool explaining to him that a prostitute made off with all he had. Gamden stopped, sat down and held his head in his hands, and said to himself, "Think Gamden, where did you put the gold!" It literally hurt to think, slowly memories came to him.

Memories such as walking into the room with a girl under his arm, and Senusret with a girl over his shoulder. The next memory was of him and the girl kissing and groping each other. She got up and went to use the chamber pot and he started to undress…

Gamden stood up and said out loud, "My boots, it's in my boots!" Running across the room he tripped over Senusret, sprawled across the floor naked and snoring. Crawling on his hands and knees the rest of the way, he reached his boots and turned them upside down, and the pouch fell to the floor with a thud, still full. Gamden rolled over onto his back holding the pouch close to his heart, thanking Zeus for his good fortune. After lying there for a good half-hour, he got to his feet again and muttered, "Never again."

While dressing, Gamden went over in his head what needed to be done before they left Khaemwaset. First on the list: go to Kefu's mansion and see him. Hopefully get some of his gadgets for the road. Next, back to Nebetah and find a ship to get them to Dionysodoros. He got up out of his chair and walked over to where Senusret still lay on the floor snoring. Nudging him with the toe of his boot, he said, "Wake up, we gotta go! C'mon let's go!" When he didn't wake up, Gamden sat on his chest. Going up and down with each deep breath, Gamden waited for him to wake up but he just kept on snoring. He rapped on Senusret's forehead with his knuckles and said again, "Wake up, we gotta go! C'mon let's go!"

Senusret opened his eyes and slowly focused on Gamden sitting on his chest, and said, "Did I ever have a good time last night. Those two girls sure were fun." He rolled over, causing Gamden to hit the floor flat on his back. Once he was standing, Senusret continued while stretching, "We gotta go back downstairs and find us a couple more girls for tonight."

Still sitting on the floor, Gamden looked up at him and said, "We can't do that."

"Why not? You got lots of coin. Maybe we can even get Qadir for the night."

Gamden held out his hand and Senusret pulled him up off the floor. "We have to get going, Senusret. Actually, we should have been at Kefu's mansion last night."

"Why, what's the big rush?"

"Don't you remember? I told you last night that we have to get to Azerta."

Senusret thought about it for a couple of seconds and said, "I had a lot to drink last night, I really don't remember anything before we got up to the room."

"You haven't changed a bit," said Gamden, with a laugh. "Now, put your clothes on and let's get going."

OK, OK, but first we should stop and get some wine for the walk."

"No way, you big bastard! You don't need no more. You drank enough wine last night to drown a horse."

Pleading with him as he put on his coat, "Just one bottle. Please, Gamden."

Gamden walked over to the door, opened it and said in a stern voice, "Get going, you big bastard. No more wasting time."

They walked out the front door of the Wild Hog into a bright sunny morning. Both Gamden and Senusret took off their coats and slung them over their haversacks. They walked to the nearest fountain, enjoying the warm sun. Filling up their water skins they also filled their bellies and enjoyed a quick wash. The entire time, Gamden kept an eye out for the city guard. It was early enough that their patrols were just starting. When he finished washing he rummaged through his sack and pulled out a hooded cloak and put it on.

"How come you're wearing that?" asked Senusret.

"Gotta keep myself hidden. Guard will be out soon."

Senusret looked around, but the street was still basically empty. "Oh, yeah! That's right, if they find you they're gonna kick yer ass into the city lockup." With a concerned tone in his voice, he continued, "Maybe you should pay me now. You know, just in case."

"Stop you're bellyachin'!" Laughed Gamden, as he locked the clasp around the neck of the cloak and drew the hood to cover his features. They avoided all the main streets on their way to the gates out of the city. Along the way they stopped for breakfast and some extra food for the walk to the mansion.

When they got to the gate, they waited a bit until the traffic in and out was steady enough that they could blend into the crowd. Outside the walls of the city, Gamden finally relaxed and removed the cloak. The inner walls of Khaemwaset had only one main gate. That meant an extra half-hour walk on top of the two to the mansion. The entire time they were walking, Senusret complained about the fact that they only had water but no wine for him to drink. There were a couple of times he almost turned back to the city, but the thought of losing all the gold and diamonds kept him walking. Finally, at the mansion, Gamden pounded on the door and shouted, "Wake up, Kefu, it's your old apprentice, Gamden!" Not a sound was heard from the old mage's home. Gamden looked at Senusret and said, "I hope the old man is all right. It has to be almost ten years since I left." Gamden pounded on the door one more time, and when he still didn't get a response he said, "Come with me, Senusret, I know a secret entrance into Kefu's home. But be careful, Kefu had many enemies and he set up traps all over the grounds. I know most of his traps and where he set them, but he is very smart and probably hid a few more since I've been gone. Just stay behind me, but not too close. I can't see the traps when I'm in your shadow, you big bastard." Gamden turned and looked up at Senusret and gave him a good shove, barely moving him.

Slowly, they made their way to the walled courtyard at the back.

" OK!" said Gamden. "Break me off a long branch from that tree behind you." Senusret turned around and snapped off a branch without effort, then handed it over. "I remember that Kefu would use the silk of a black widow to make wire from. So thin it's almost invisible but strong enough to cut through skin and bone." Gamden held on to the branch as he draped it over the top of the wall. A finger length above the wall, the branch seemed to stop in mid-air. "There it is!" chuckled Gamden. "Watch this!" He pulled back on the branch and they heard the wire snap. From the top of the post at the other end of the wall, a blowgun ejected a poisoned dart that stuck into the branch. "Everything in this place can be dangerous!"

Senusret nodded his head and repeated, "Dangerous, got it!"

"C'mon over here," Gamden said, as he pointed to a specific spot. "Stand against the wall so I can climb up on your shoulders and get into the courtyard." Senusret backed up against the wall, bent over and formed a stirrup by weaving his fingers together. Gamden stepped into the stirrup and braced himself against Senusret's shoulders, ready to climb over the fence, nice and slow.

One, two, three!" counted down Senusret, and on three he launched Gamden over the wall, clearing it by at least four hands. Gamden landed on the other side with a thud. Senusret stood where he was, laughing so hard he was doubled over.

"That wasn't funny!" shouted Gamden, as he lay on the ground in pain. That only made Senusret laugh even harder, until he was crying. "I'm serious, that really hurt, you big bastard!"

Senusret composed himself, then scaled the wall easily, landing beside Gamden. "You don't look hurt," said Senusret, as he reached down and picked him up under the arms, standing him on his feet. "Let me dust you off!" Giving him a few good pats on the back, dust billowed from Gamden's clothes. "There, good as new."

"Thanks, I think," squeaked Gamden, in discomfort. "OK, let's get going." Gamden led the way, limping as he went.

Three more disarmed traps and one close call later, they made it to the back door. "Finally, we made it," said Senusret. "I hope he has some wine in there, I'm so thirsty I've got cactus sprouting on my tongue." Senusret reached for the door latch.

"No! Don't do that!" shouted Gamden, and he lunged forward to grab his arm. But it was too late. Senusret tried to slide the lock open, when he did there was a loud click. Lightning sprang from the rune painted on the door and struck Senusret in the chest.

With a look of disbelief, Gamden asked, "are you OK, Senusret? You look a little singed."

In a voice barely audible, Senusret asked, "What was that?" Then fell face-first into the door. A smell of burnt clothing filled the air around them from the massive discharge of electricity. "You big bastard," Gamden said out loud. "Thanks for finding that trap, but now how am I supposed to get inside when you are blocking the door." Looking around, he found a small tree that had fallen near them and used it to lever him away from the door. With a crash, Senusret fell over unconscious in the bushes. Gamden tried the door but it was still locked. Going through his haversack, he found a ring full of old skeleton keys that he had made over the years. After trying several different keys, he found the one that worked. Gamden opened the door and walked into a solarium full of dead and dying plants. "Kefu!" shouted Gamden. "Kefu, are you here? Where are you?"

The mansion was dark and felt empty, as if nothing or no one had moved there in weeks. "I don't like this one bit," he said to himself, as he went into the main sitting room. The doors of the library to his left were closed and Gamden was taking no chances. He checked the door for a trap but found nothing. Inside the room were the decaying remains of Kefu. His skeleton was still sitting up in his reading chair.

"What got you first, old man?" Gamden asked the skeleton. "Old age or an enemy?" Gamden thoroughly searched the corpse. "Can't find any stab wounds and your skull is in one piece. Old age it was that got you then, or maybe poison?" Another search of the garments turned up a small bag of coins and a key. "I was hoping that you were going to have this key on you. Saves me the trouble of picking that lock on your old chest or having to rummage through this big house where you have a million hiding places."

Senusret came around the corner with a bottle of wine in each hand. "What happened out there? The last thing that I remember was trying to open the door."

"It's a good thing you're such a big bastard," said Gamden. "You sprung one of Kefu's traps. You took a lightening bolt to the chest. Somebody my size would be cooked and dead. Guess I should thank you for disarming it."

"Why are we here, anyway?" asked Senusret. "If we took such a big risk in coming here, there must be something you want really bad. Is it money?"

"What we came here for will be much more important to us," said Gamden. "We need to find a ratty old chest. Kefu was never very clean and he would forget where he would put things, even something as valuable as his chest. It could be anywhere in this house."

Two hours and several bottles of wine later, they found the chest buried in the back of a closet on the second level. They cleared a spot on the floor and set the chest down. Carefully, Gamden looked the chest over to make sure that Kefu hadn't set a trap on the chest too. It looked clean and Gamden was about to put the key in the lock, when he hesitated and said, "This is too easy. The trap is that it's too easy. We need to take the chest outside." Gamden tried to pick the chest up but couldn't. "Senusret, can you carry this outside for me?" Senusret finished off the bottle of wine in one gulp, belched and picked the chest up like a sack of rags.

When they had the chest in the back courtyard. Gamden hacked down a small tree and stripped the branches off. Once that was done, he took a Y-shaped branch and drove it firmly in the ground. Then he tied the key to the end of the tree and laid it into the Y-shaped stick. Gamden then counted the paces from the chest to the end of the small tree.

"I counted twenty paces," said Gamden. "I think we should be safe."

"Safe from what?" asked Senusret.

"Kefu was a very smart mage. I think that the trap goes off when you put the key in the lock."

"More lightning?" asked Senusret.

"Who knows, Kefu forgot more than I know, and he still knew twice as much as I do now. I don't know what to use on the trap to disarm it, so its going off no matter what and I want to be a safe distance away when it does."

Gamden slowly guided the key into the lock and turned it. There was a soft click as the lock opened and then a loud click as the trap went off. A billowing green cloud exploded from the lock. In a split second the cloud reached the two of them. Senusret reacted even faster. He picked Gamden up with one arm and threw him twenty paces. Then with one leap, he landed right beside him. Everything the cloud touched was killed by acid.

"See what I mean?" said Gamden. "I forgot that he could do that, acid cloud, very nasty."

"Acid cloud." repeated Senusret as he nodded. "Very nasty."

"Well, Senusret we need to wait for that cloud to dissipate. Let's go find a bottle of wine." Gamden and Senusret walked out of the house a few minutes later, each with a bottle of wine. The wind had finally dissipated the acid cloud. All the foliage within the radius of the cloud had been killed, and many birds, insects and other wildlife littered the ground, either killed in the trees or where they stood in the long grass. It was a good thing that the lock on the chest opened before the trap went off. The iron key was mostly melted away and had become fused with the lock. The two looked at each other and decided to go look at the chest.

"Is it safe now? asked Senusret. That was a nasty trap, do you think there is another inside?"

I sure hope not," replied Gamden. "Old Kefu was crafty and could make incredible little devices. Almost all of them deadly and very difficult to detect."

"If this old Kefu made such dangerous things, why do you still want to look inside?" Senusret asked.

"This is why!" Gamden opened the chest and inside were books, scrolls and strange looking contraptions of all sorts, shapes and sizes. "Senusret, hold open this bag for me so I can pick the things that we need for our travels."

Gamden looked at all the scrolls and books. He took a few books and most of the scrolls. Near the bottom of the chest he found six items in particular that he liked.

"See these, Senusret? They're grenades!"

"I've never seen anything like them," said Senusret. "What do they do?"

"Kefu was talking about making these out of iron, looks like he finally did it." Gamden pointed at the grenade and said, "You light this fuse at the top and throw it at your enemy. Then you run or find cover. There is an explosive inside this, BOOM! Kills a lot of enemies at the same time."

"Sounds like we are going to be doing a lot of fighting on this quest," said Senusret. "I think I should get more money for this."

"Don't worry about it." Gamden reached up and put his hand on Senusret's shoulder. "With these scrolls and inventions of Kefu's we won't have any problems."

"What is on those scrolls that you took anyway?" Senusret pointed at the bag on the ground.

"Mostly magic spells and maps of the distant lands that we are going to travel through. Now let's hide the rest of the books and other things in the house. We have a lot more to do today other than steal and drink."

"What do you mean?" shouted Senusret. "I'm starving, and some more wine would be perfect right now."

"Let's compromise then, you big hungry bastard," answered Gamden. "We go through the market on our way to the docks for passage across the sea."

"It's a deal!"

6

Gamden and Senusret walked up the stairs from the cellar where they had hidden the rest of the books and gadgets. Turning the corner into the kitchen, they saw a man just as tall as Gamden but with wider shoulders, thickly muscled and wearing a green helmet and armour. He had a sword in one hand and a round green shield in the other. "Halt!" shouted the man. "What have you done with Kefu?"

Senusret reached for his sword, but Gamden was faster and stopped him. "My name is Gamden. I was a student of Kefu for many years. I stopped in to seek assistance and guidance from my former master. Who are you?"

When the stranger heard Gamden's name, he relaxed and sheathed his sword. "My name is Akhom, I am a warrior priest of Athena. You probably don't remember me, but I remember you. I have been stopping at Kefu's mansion every winter solstice for many years to bring him the ingredients for his potions and spells." Removing his helmet revealed his light brown eyes full of a lifetime of wisdom, a long straight nose, close cropped hair and a narrow face. "When I entered the compound, I saw the disarmed traps and the remnants of the chest. I knew that something was wrong. Is Kefu all right?"

Gamden stepped forward and offered his arm in a friendly gesture. Akhom returned the gesture in a friendly embrace.

"I have bad news for you, my friend," Gamden said, in a sad tone. "When we got here Kefu was already dead. By the state of the decomposition of his body he could have been dead for several weeks to months. I can't tell what killed him, or if *someone* killed him."

"Where is the body?" asked Akhom.

"We left him where we found him. In the Library, follow me."

"No need," said Akhom. "I know my way, thank you."

Akhom walked past Gamden and went straight for the library.

Senusret bent down to whisper into Gamden's ear: "I don't like priests and I don't like this one even more."

"Keep it to yourself," Gamden muttered back. "I kind of remember this person now and the thing I remember most is that he truly is a warrior. Kefu had me spar with him in the courtyard, I still have the scars to prove it."

Gamden and Senusret made their way to the library. Akhom was kneeling beside the body of Kefu, praying to Athena. Taking Kefu's rotting hand in his, Akhom continued praying.

"What is he doing?" asked Senusret.

"I'm not sure," answered Gamden. "This is a kind of magic that I have never seen before."

"Gamden, find me some myrrh, quickly. I must anoint Kefu, find it in the apothecary!" barked Akhom.

Quickly, Gamden got his bearings and remembered which room it was. In no time flat, he returned with a large flask in hand.

"Hurry, pour some on his chest, over the heart, and some down his throat. I can't let go of his hand if this is going to work."

Gamden hesitated for a moment, gripped with revulsion at having to touch Kefu's corpse.

"I said hurry!" shouted Akhom. "This has to work the first time, there is no second chance!"

Gamden ripped open the nightshirt and poured the myrrh over the chest, and then forced the jaw open and guided the neck of the flask into the mouth, spilling most but getting some down what was left of the throat. The flask slipped out of Gamden's hand and shattered on the floor. Akhom concentrated on his task. He stopped praying, and with his free hand traced the outline of a rune in the myrrh on the chest of the corpse. The rune took on a light blue color. Seconds later one of the fingers on the corpse moved.

"Good." said Akhom. "Kefu, can you hear me? Tell me what happened to you. It's your old friend, Akhom. Kefu, can you hear me?"

The corpse moved its head to look at Akhom with empty eye sockets. In a whispered voice, the corpse of Kefu answered without moving the jawbone: "Akhom, you are late. Why are you late?"

"That's not important," answered Akhom. "Kefu, tell me what happened to you. How did you die?"

"Oh...am I dead? How long have I been dead for?"

"That's not important. Kefu, what is the last thing that you remember?"

The corpse looked off into space for a moment, and then said, "The last thing I remember was sitting in my library smoking my pipe, drinking my wine and enjoying the sun with my familiar. Where is my familiar?" Seconds later, a large black male cat with bright yellow eyes jumped on the lap of the Kefu, purring, tail in the air. The corpse petted the cat affectionately and sighed, content. "That is the last thing that I remember."

"Kefu, it's me, Gamden. Do you remember me?"

"Of course I remember you, boy," the corpse said, extending a bony arm and looking directly at Gamden with its empty eye sockets. "Take my hand, Gamden. Just for a moment."

Gamden hesitated and looked at Akhom for guidance.

Akhom nodded and said, "Take his hand, Gamden. He wants to give you his familiar. Don't deny him this!"

Slowly, Gamden reached out and took his hand. The corpse took his with a firm grasp and said, "Take good care of my familiar, his name is Khepri, he will be your eyes and ears in places you cannot go." Letting go of Gamden's hand, he began to pet the cat and continued: "Gamden, pet Khepri with me." Gamden reached out to pet him, Khepri smelled his fingers then rubbed his head on Gamden's hand. "You belong to Gamden now. Take care of him and serve your new master well." Khepri looked up into its empty eye sockets and let out a long, loud meow, then jumped down to sit next to Gamden and groomed himself.

"Kefu, look at me," said Akhom. "We have to go now, old friend. I will miss our talks around the fire."

"I will miss you, too, I always looked forward to your visits." The corpse reached up with its bony hand and tugged on Gamden's sleeve. "I loved you as a son and I still do today. You have my permission to take what you need from my home. Goodbye, son."

With that, Akhom let go of Kefu's hand. The rune on its chest lost its colour and the head fell back.

Akhom stood and said, "We must build a funeral pyre for Kefu. He was far too powerful of a mage to let his physical body remain. Necromancers are few and far between, but if any of them knew of Kefu's corpse, they could reanimate him and he would have to do their bidding."

"But *you* reanimated his corpse," said Senusret." Are you a necromancer?"

"I did not reanimate Kefu. All I did was contact his spirit, Kefu could only answer simple questions and could barely move." Akhom walked across the room and pulled a large book from one of the shelves. He put it down and opened it to a series of fine hand-drawn pictures and script, describing how to raise the dead in all states of decay. "A powerful necromancer can use the magic within Kefu. He was so old and had used magic almost all his life that his body has become imbued with it."

"Very dangerous," said Gamden.

"Very dangerous," repeated Akhom.

"Now I have to prepare Kefu's body," said Akhom. "Gamden, why don't you and Senusret go and get us a pheasant or two for supper. Talking to Kefu has been a drain on my body. After we eat, then we will build his pyre."

7

Gamden and Senusret walked outside and around the back of the mansion to the cellar. They rummaged through every nook and cranny and found a short bow marked with indecipherable runes, plus a quiver of arrows.

Beyond the walls of Kefu's mansion, Gamden and Senusret slowly walked the path leading into the forest, constantly looking for their dinner. "Akhom may be a priest and a pompous prick," said Senusret, "but he seems to have been a good friend of Kefu's, and if he was your master as a boy, you turned out all right. I guess I can trust Akhom."

"You're right," answered Gamden. "He is both of those things, but now that I have had time to think, I do remember Akhom more now. Kefu always greeted Akhom with friendship and he was always welcome to come and go as he pleased."

"Did Akhom really train you as a warrior when you were here?" asked Senusret. "I always thought you were just a terrible thief."

Gamden stopped, turned and motioned for Senusret to bend down to look him in the eye.

"First off," stated Gamden, "you big bastard, I'm a *great* thief! Second, I was trained by Akhom and I will pin your ears back if you're not careful. And lastly, the other thing I didn't tell you is that Kefu taught me how to use magic, maybe tonight in your sleep I will turn you into an ugly toad. Probably be an improvement!"

For a moment, Senusret had a genuine look of concern, then he laughed and said, "Out of my way. My dinner is out there somewhere and I'm getting hungry." Senusret pushed his way past and continued walking down the path. "Come on, these pheasants might be too much for me. I might need the help of the mighty warrior Gamden."

"Shut up, you big bastard!" shouted Gamden, and with a smile he started after him.

A little while longer and a bit further down the path, Gamden said, "It is getting late in the day, and with the winter solstice here the sun will set soon."

"I think I'm going to starve to death," answered Senusret.

"Stop for a moment." Gamden looked through his pack and pulled out a metal tube. "I almost forgot that I had this in my pack. It's a spyglass."

"What does it do?" asked Senusret.

"It makes things that are far away look like they are at arm's length." Gamden expanded the spyglass and brought it into focus. "Try it. You bring it up to your eye and look through it." Gamden demonstrated, then handed it over.

Senusret looked through it. "Amazing," he mumbled. Looking a little off to the left, he saw a group of pheasants. He lowered the spyglass. "I can't see them without this thing. Amazing."

Quietly, they continued up the path, trying not to spook their prey. "Let's take cover behind the tree up there." Gamden pointed to the bend in the path.

"I still can't see them." Senusret kneeled down by the tree, looked through the spyglass and focused it. Slowly scanning the horizon, he whispered, "There they are," pointing off to the left and handing the spyglass over.

"I see them too. Who's the better shot?" asked Gamden.

"I couldn't hit an elephant from here," answered Senusret. Gamden readied his shortbow, drew the arrow, took aim and released. The arrow leapt silently from the bow with the speed of lightning. Gamden and Senusret looked at each other for a moment. Firing another arrow into the nye caused them to scatter. When they reached the pheasants, the arrows were nowhere to be seen, but the dead pheasants had perfect kill shots and the wounds were cauterized.

"Let's go," said Senusret. "I'm starving, and these are nice fat birds. Can't wait to roast them up and have some wine."

"Always thinking with your stomach, Senusret, but this time I agree. Let's go." Gamden hesitated for a moment looking for the arrows, with no luck. "I can't find those two arrows anywhere."

"So what?" answered Senusret.

"So what?" continued Gamden. "This is most likely a magical bow of some kind." Gamden looked closely at the bow as they made their way back to the mansion. "These runes must have something to do with it, very faint and I don't recognize the language. When we get back to the mansion I will have to decipher them."

"Talk, talk, talk. That's all you do," said Senusret. "All I want to do is eat and drink until I can't drink no more! C'mon, I'll race you back."

8

When they returned to the mansion, Senusret stayed outside and started to prepare the pheasants for roasting. Gamden went inside and looked for Akhom. He found him in the library, sitting on the floor. When Gamden stepped in, he said, "What took you so long, I thought you got lost."

"I thought you were asleep, so no need to hurry, right?" answered Gamden.

"I heard you come in the door. Poor excuse for a thief, I think." Gamden said nothing. "Yes, Kefu and I kept tabs on you. He thought highly of you. Best pupil he ever taught."

"He never told me that," replied Gamden.

"Well, he did, now help me send him to the gods."

Akhom gestured toward the body of Kefu. He had taken care to wash the corpse and anoint it with precious oils. Then he had wrapped it in clean cloth on which he had written essentials prayers to help Kefu take his place among the gods.

"Kefu said there was something unique about you," continued Akhom. "He had never seen anyone else learn and use magic so easily. He wanted you to stay but you ran off in the night before he could talk to you."

"I didn't want to hurt him…I couldn't talk to him," stuttered Gamden. "He wouldn't have understood."

"He loved you like a son," replied Akhom. "He never told you how you came into his life?"

"I asked him many times," replied Gamden. "But he would always change the subject or say that it wasn't time for me to know."

"Kefu wanted to wait until you were sixteen, Gamden, but you left on your fourteenth birthday. Kefu never took on another student after you left. He thought that he failed the gods who brought you to him and was no longer worthy to serve them," replied Akhom.

"I was so angry, I had to leave the mansion. He wouldn't tell me who I was!" blurted Gamden. "I knew he wasn't my father. He was so old, I could just tell."

"Pick up the corpse and carry it outside, Gamden, and I will tell you what I was told." As they left the library, Akhom began his tale. "Kefu was alone on a stormy summer night when there was a loud knock on the front door. When he answered the door, a tall, cloaked figure was standing in the rain. The stranger said, 'This child needs a good home, Master Kefu.' The figure opened his cloak to reveal a child wrapped in swaddling garments. 'Love him and teach him as if he were your own.' Kefu asked the figure who he was and where he came from, but all he would say is that the child was a gift from the gods who was not to know his true lineage until he was sixteen years old."

Akhom and Gamden walked out of the mansion into the main courtyard, where Senusret was busy roasting the pheasants over a small fire.

"Those birds almost ready now?" asked Akhom. Senusret looked up with a mouthful of meat and nodded his head in agreement. "I'm ready for a good meal. Gamden, put the corpse on the cairn behind you and then come eat."

While they ate, Akhom explained more of the reasons why Kefu could not tell Gamden where he came from. "Can you forgive him, Gamden?"

"Yes, now I can. I'm older now and I have learned so much on my own, I can understand the conflict that was in Kefu's heart everyday. He loved me as a son, I do remember that."

"That makes me happy." Akhom stood up from where he was sitting near the fire and wiped the supper from around his mouth.

"Gamden, I need your help, and your friend's, too. We need to build a funeral pyre to send Kefu to his rightful place next to the gods. Last year when I was here I cut a lot of the old growth down in the main courtyard and piled it by the old stables. Help me bring the wood over." On the way to the stables, Akhom continued, "Gamden, there is something else that you should know about your time with Kefu. He saw that you used magic very easily. Almost as if it were a part of you from birth and that your mastery of magic would make you powerful one day."

Senusret laughed out loud, and said, "All this time you have been masquerading as a terrible thief."

Gamden threw a large stick and hit Senusret in the chest.

"Now that I have found you again, Gamden, I intend to continue your magic training. Kefu showed me the texts that he wanted you to learn. My knowledge of magic is nowhere near that of Kefu, but I will do my best."

"I'm afraid that will not be possible, Akhom. Senusret and me need to be on our way first thing tomorrow."

"Then I will come with you," said Akhom. "I gave my word to Kefu and I mean to follow through with it."

"We are on a job that will take us to Azerta," said Gamden. "I can't pay you for your services and the journey will be perilous."

"I know the road to Azerta well, and my payment will be fulfilling my word to Kefu."

Gamden and Senusret looked at each other, and they both knew it would be best if Akhom were to join them.

"Welcome to our party." Senusret took Akhom's hand in friendship.

The last pieces of wood were put down to finish the pyre. Akhom picked up the corpse and placed it gently on top. Then he took out a small dagger and made a cut across his right hand. He began to write sacred runes in his own blood on the funeral shroud and softly sing hymns. When he was finished, Akhom bandaged his hand and said, "Kefu is ready, I have prepared his corpse in the time-honoured ways. The gods will be pleased and will let him sit with them for all eternity."

Just as Akhom finished what he was saying, Khepri jumped up on the pyre and laid a freshly-killed mouse on the funeral shroud, meowed loudly then jumped down to Gamden's feet, purring.

Akhom took a burning log from the cooking fire and lit the pyre.

When the fire took hold of the wood and began to burn hot, the runes that Akhom had placed on the shroud began to glow brilliant blue, and did so until the corpse was completely burned.

"The night is late," said Akhom. "If we have an early start tomorrow we will need our sleep to make the best of the short winter days. Let's sleep in Kefu's house one last time."

9

The next morning was not quite as early a start as was hoped. Senusret stayed up most of the night drinking the last of the wine in Kefu's house. When he did finally wake up he wouldn't set foot out of the mansion without breakfast.

"A man my size needs to eat whenever he can, and right now I have to eat to get rid of this pounding headache. What was in that wine?"

"It's not what was in that wine," answered Akhom, "but how old the wine was. Kefu hadn't had a drop of wine in nearly five years. I remember helping him prepare that year's grape harvest. It was the last time we did that. Excellent growing year that was." Akhom stopped and thought for a moment. "I think Kefu had some vials of quick healing in his chemist store room. Should help with your obvious alcohol poisoning."

"I didn't drink that much," said Senusret, as Akhom walked out of the room. "Did I really drink that much last night, Gamden?"

"Let me put it to you this way, Kefu had a full wine closet when we got here the other day."

"Yeah, so what's your point?" asked Senusret.

"The point is that there was twenty-five bottles in the closet and now it's empty. Lucky you're such a big bastard. If I had drank that much I would be dead on the floor with coins in my mouth for the Charon."

Senusret shook his head and said, "I couldn't help myself, the wine was so good, not like that swill that we drink back home."

"Kefu grew the finest grapes in all the three kingdoms. I remember eating them off the vine in the summer," answered Akhom, as he walked back into the room. "Gamden is right, you should be dead. I have only seen a couple other men your size in my entire life, back when I went into the southern jungles beyond the Al Sabal cliffs. Have you lived all your life in the three kingdoms, Senusret?"

"No, I have vague memories of traveling with my father as a boy from our village in the South," replied Senusret. "My mother died when I was very young from the plagues. That's why we came to the three kingdoms, to get away from the wars and the disease that followed."

"Where you come from, Senusret, there is a potent drink fermented from the root of a tree. That is most likely where you get your high tolerance for alcohol. Drink this vial of quick healing and you will feel better."

Senusret took the vial from Akhom and drank it all down in one mouthful.

"You will be ready to travel in a few minutes," said Akhom. "Lay back and rest while Gamden and me go into the library and find what I need to continue his training." They walked into the library and Akhom continued, "Look for scrolls that contain Kefu's handwriting in the ancient script, they will contain spells for controlling the elements. There is also a large book in a faded red leather cover that has everything I need to teach you advanced offensive and defensive spells."

"What about my new…" Gamden hesitated, then continued, "my familiar. Isn't that what Kefu called the cat?"

"This new familiar will be the right hand you never knew you lost." Akhom stopped what he was doing, looked at Gamden and said in a matter-of-fact tone, "Khepri will be your best friend. He will go into places that you can't. You will see through his eyes and hear what goes on around him. Treat him well and he will save your life many times over." Akhom walked over to a pile of scrolls on the corner table. He sorted through them and took three of them.

"That, too, we will learn in these scrolls."

"How do you know all these things, Akhom?"

"I have known Kefu for most of my life, Gamden. Not only was he my friend, but he was my master as well."

"But you are such a powerful warrior," Gamden said, with surprised tone. "What could Kefu be able to teach you?"

"Yes, I am a powerful warrior, and the teachings of my order give me strengths that allow me to defeat my enemies, but Kefu taught me how to defend myself without taking human life."

"Why do you carry a sword, then?" asked Gamden.

"More often than not, just the sight of the weapon can stop a foe in his tracks," said Akhom, as he pulled the sword from its sheath. "But there are also times when the taking of life can't be helped."

They finished looking through the library and found several more items they needed. As they walked out into the kitchen they found Senusret lying on his back in the middle of the floor, sleeping. His snoring was so loud that with each breath he made the crystal vases in the cabinets along the wall rattle.

"By Athena!" shouted Akhom, over the snoring. "That boy is a monster, isn't he? Everything about him is big, even his snoring!"

"He is a big bastard!" shouted Gamden. "But he is my most trusted friend, he has saved my skin too many times to count"

Akhom picked up a large clay pitcher and filled it with water from the hand pump. He walked over to where Senusret lay on the floor and poured the water over his face. Senusret sat up in a flash, spitting and sputtering water everywhere.

"Why did you wake me up?!" shouted Senusret. "I was having the best dream. Just me in a room surrounded by women, all the wine I could drink, and I was just finishing with the women!" Then he stopped and thought for a second. "I feel so much better now. What was in that vial? I feel like I could take on the cyclops monarch myself."

"I learned many healing techniques from Kefu," said Akhom. "But I could never match his skills. The effects of the potion will last at least a week. Cuts and bruises will heal rapidly, and you won't need sleep for at least two days."

"Two days without sleep!" shouted Senusret. "What am I supposed to do?"

Gamden laughed, and said, "You can think about not drinking all the wine in someone's house, you big bastard. Now let's get going to Nebetah."

10

When they walked out to the stables by the guesthouse of Kefu's mansion, there was a short bald man in grey traveling vestments standing there, holding a walking stick twice his height. His interest was in a scroll that was rolled out before him. His back was turned, and he held up a finger that stopped the three in their tracks. They looked at each other.

"I know you're there," he said. "I just need to finish reading this fascinating scroll on alchemy."

"Who are you!?" asked Akhom.

He continued to read with his finger in the air, mumbling the words as he read at a lightning-fast speed.

"Finished!" he said, then rolled up the scroll and turned to face them.

"My name is Menkaure. I am the head cleric at the monastery of Hermes." Big white eyes dominated Menkaure's appearance. Wrinkles creased every which way across the leathered skin on his face. Small nose and thin lips filled in the rest of his tiny features.

"Why are you here?" asked Gamden.

"Kefu told me to come here," replied Menkaure.

"You lie!" said Akhom, as he lay his hand on the hilt of his sword. "Kefu is dead!"

"Yes, I know," answered Menkaure softly, as he bowed his head in a quick prayer. "Two weeks ago, Kefu came to me in a dream."

"That means nothing," growled Akhom.

"Kefu was an old friend of mine," pleaded Menkaure. "Kefu must have mentioned me, maybe by my name before I became a cleric of the Amunet monastery. Khafra was my name then. We were practically brothers."

Akhom relaxed and said, "Yes, Kefu did mention you numerous times. Although he never did mention how short you are." All three of them towered over Menkaure.

"My physical stature is not my strength. No, my mind is my strength. I never forget anything I've ever read or any conversation with any person or any place I've ever been."

"You said that Kefu came to you in dream?" asked Gamden.

"Yes, he did, Gamden."

"How do you know my name?"

"Kefu told me all about you in my dream, but he never mentioned you." Menkaure pointed at Senusret.

Senusret reached down and picked Menkaure up so he could look him in the eyes, and said, "You're smart, eh, with my brawn we could rule the world!" Senusret laughed and put him down.

Menkaure straightened his vestment and continued on about his dream, "Kefu also told me that I should follow you on your quest. If I did, I would be witness to miraculous events."

"What does that mean?" asked Gamden.

" I have no idea. He was elusive about the details."

"Kefu could be clairvoyant, and as the years passed his powers became keener," added Akhom.

"Yes, his magic was powerful," continued Menkaure. "I corresponded with him through the monastery courier. I've been cloistered there for most of my adult life."

"Is that why you are of such small stature?" asked Gamden.

"That's right, my life is purely academic. Everything is done for me so that my mind can record everything it can."

"How old are you, then?" asked Gamden.

"I have lived for eight generations and would like eight more. Praise Hermes!" Menkaure raised his arms to the air.

"If you're so old, how did you get to Khaemwaset?" asked Senusret.

Menkaure gave a loud whistle. Within a few seconds, a large saddled horse, laden with many large leather pouches and small wooden crates, came out of the stables. The horse walked with long, silent strides right up to Menkaure and stopped. The horse lowered its muzzle for the treat it expected and got a piece of apple.

"This is my trusted steed and best friend. Her name is Merit, I raised her from a foal. When my days are full of learning I can always count on her to take my mind away from the library and escape to the stables."

"How do you get onto your horse? Even the stirrup is above your head," pointed out Senusret.

"Easy," said Menkaure, with a smile. He took his walking stick, and with the hook on the end he unbuckled a small rope ladder that came to the ground at his feet. In a few seconds Menkaure was in the saddle, ladder rolled up and secured.

All three laughed with amazement at the speed the small Menkaure displayed.

When he was finished laughing, Akhom said, "Why don't you take point on the trail to Nebetah. We'll get my horse and catch up to you in a few minutes."

"A horse!" blurted Gamden. "I need a horse! I'm not walking all the way to Azerta."

"We can fix that," answered Akhom.

"Let's get going, Merit. These slowpokes can meet us in Nebetah." Merit neighed and started down the wooded path, as Menkaure sang his favorite traveling song.

Akhom turned to the open field behind the stables. He put two fingers in his mouth, and with all his might whistled three times. From the other side of the field at the tree line, a young black colt came running at full speed, large clumps of dirt flying from its hooves. It reached them in a few seconds.

"How did you know that horse was there?" Gamden asked, with amazement.

"Two years back I was on my way to see Kefu when I came across a mare that had died while birthing that beautiful animal right there," answered Akhom. "I cleaned him up and carried him the rest of the way here. Kefu and I nursed him back to health and trained him." The colt tried its best to slow down, but in the excitement of seeing Akhom again, almost bowled him over.

"This is Naudar!" said Akhom as he wrapped his arms around the horse's neck and held on for dear life. Every muscle rippled in Naudar's body from the exertion of the run across the field.

"Wow, what a horse!" said Senusret, wide-eyed with amazement. Gamden was speechless and could only nod in agreement.

When Naudar finally came to a complete stop, Akhom laughed out loud and said, "I've missed you too, boy!" Snorting and stomping, Naudar wouldn't calm down until Akhom took him by the ears, looked him in the eye and spoke in an unfamiliar language. Naudar visibly calmed down and remembered his training. "Good boy! Now go in the stable and find your saddle."

"Come, Gamden, let's get him ready for the road."

11

The road to the port city of Nebetah was easy travelling for the four companions. Unlike the cargo trail that Gamden was spirited into the city on, the main road was wide and not as steep. Bright sunlight warmed the party as they made their way to the port. The byway was busy with merchant caravans and people from all corners of the three kingdoms. Slaves from the eastern wildlands made up the bulk of the cargo of the horse-drawn carts that travel to Khaemwaset.

"I hate to see the slave traders and their carts," said Senusret. "When I was a boy we always lived with the fear that one day the slavers would come to our village and take us away. The warlords constantly raided villages for slaves to feed their armies."

"You never told me about stuff like that," said Gamden. "And I have known you most of your life."

"I don't remember too much about my life in the Southlands, mostly that it was hot and I was sick all the time."

Hiding his emotions, Senusret laughed and turned away from the distant stares of the slaves in the cavalcade.

"I hate slavery too, Senusret. Kefu and I also had to run from the slavers," said Menkaure. "That was back when the King brothers set out to bring peace to the fractured city states. That was where Kefu and I came to be in the employ of Ahmose, who later took Kefu as a mage apprentice and sent me off to Amunet Monastery."

"I can't believe this!" Gamden ejaculated, with amazement. "I lived with Kefu until I was in my teens and have known Senusret since my teens. I'm finding out all this stuff about you two. Almost like meeting you for the first time."

"Kefu was very old, Gamden. He was a father when he rescued me from certain death," continued Menkaure. "I am one hundred and fifty years old and feel like I could live that much more again. Praise Hermes!" Menkaure raised his hands to the heavens.

"How did you two live so long?" asked Senusret. "My father only lived until he was forty, I'm in my twenties now, how can I live as long as you?"

"Kefu lived as long as he did because he used magic all his life. When a person uses magic that long it becomes a part of their body and soul. It extends life and gives clarity of thought."

"You don't use magic, yet you are almost as old as Kefu was?" asked Gamden. "What's your secret?"

"I can cast spells by reading from a scroll, but that is not enough for magic to become a part of me; rather, I was blessed by the prophet Hatshepsut. She is the oldest of us, even she doesn't remember how many generations she has lived."

"I have seen her as well," interjected Akhom. "She is wise beyond anyone else in all the three kingdoms."

At that moment, the party of four rounded the final corner before Nebetah and the city spread out before them, leading to the Neferkare Sea. Farms ringed the city, growing the crops that fed the people and was used for trade with the eastern wildlands. The harbour was full of ships of all kinds, with many more waiting to dock.

"That's a sight for sore eyes," said Senusret.

"Do you have friends and family here?" asked Menkaure.

"No, I just remember there being a few good pubs along the docks where we can drink tonight!"

"Senusret, stop thinking with your stomach," said Akhom, with a frown. "We won't have time for that. As soon as we get to the docks we need to get provisions for our travels. Then find a ship for passage to Dionysodoros."

"I'm not going nowhere without wine," said Senusret, and he stopped dead in his tracks in the middle of the road. "If there ain't no wine where we're going then I'm not going anywhere!"

"C'mon Senusret, I need your help on this job," pleaded Gamden.

"No way! No wine, no job!"

"I think I have a solution to our problem," interjected Menkaure. I have some very potent hashish in my pack."

"What is that?" asked Senusret.

"Have you ever smoked marijuana?"

"Yes, I have, many times, and it does nothing for me!"

"I think you will be surprised with what I have here to stuff in my pipe. Come to Nebetah and I promise to get you more intoxicated than your wine will ever make you."

Senusret looked like he was having a very important conversation with himself over whether or not he should go with them or stay and drown himself in wine.

"C'mon Senusret, don't be an ass! I need your help with this job."

"If I don't get loaded off this hashish of yours, Menkaure, you three are on your own!"

Menkaure started to reply, but Gamden blurted out, "It's a deal!"

Senusret looked at the two of them with concern and walked past them towards Nebetah.

Gamden leaned toward Menkaure and asked, "This hashish of yours is as good as you say it is, isn't it? If it isn't, he's outta here, you know that. He really can't live without his wine."

"This will put him in his place and shut his mouth, no worries there. I make it myself from the plants that I have growing in my own garden."

Akhom rode up to them laughing, and said, "Poor Senusret, he is in for a rude awakening. I know of hashish and how potent it can be. We might want to take extra provisions for Senusret or he will eat all our food in the first few days."

All of them laughed together and rode off to catch Senusret.

12

The four travelers entered Nebetah, and as always, the city was crowded with people of every culture and colour. The smell of the city was overpowering, it was a mix of fish, manure and coal. Not only was Nebetah a port city, but livestock was held in the city for auction and for slaughter. The blacksmiths and potteries belched out black smoke from their coal-fired furnaces, adding to the noxious stench.

The nobility was far away from the city and the crush of people. Even though the spires of the cathedrals and castles were a half hour ride out of the city, they loomed large on the horizon. Encircled by a high wall and guarded at all times, only the elite entered that part of the city.

Just outside the old city walls, Akhom stopped the group and asked, "I know we all would like to have a bed to sleep in, but I think we all can easily agree that we should sleep outside the city tonight. We want to keep a low profile, and the four of us together stick out like sore thumbs." He pointed at Gamden and Senusret. "You two find a place for us to camp tonight, preferably down wind of the city."

"And build a fire, nice and warm!" interjected Menkaure. "I am old, and my bones hurt when I get cold. Do this for me and I will bring you back a bottle of wine."

"Make it three and you got a deal," said Senusret. "Sounds like I will be thirsty when I'm finished all this work for you."

"One bottle of wine and a bowl full of hashish," countered Menkaure.

Senusret thought it over for a second and said, "Deal!"

They split into two groups, Senusret and Gamden went off to make camp, and all the way Senusret complained that he was only going to get one bottle of wine for his troubles. Gamden laughed at him and said, "Quit your bitching! Just like an old lady, bitch, bitch, bitch!"

"Shut up, Gamden!" Senusret punched him in the arm so Gamden punched him back. That is the way they continued off into the distance.

"Do you think that Senusret is worth the risk of taking with us?" asked Menkaure, as they watched them leave.

"Senusret is loyal to Gamden," replied Akhom. "I can sense that he would protect him with his own life if it came down to it."

Menkaure took one last look at them riding away, turned his horse towards the city and said, "Let's pray that we don't have to find out."

Akhom and Menkaure rode into the city and were over-whelmed by the sheer amount of people on the streets of Nebetah. Anything you wanted could be found there. All the trade of the three seas came through Nebetah. Merchants on the street and in their shops shouted to the masses, enticing them to come and buy their wares. Looking for the businesses that had dry goods for the long trip across the Neferkare Sea, they made their way through the streets. Near the centre of the trading district they passed by a large fountain where people gathered freely to talk and quench their thirst.

When Menkaure neared the fountain, a middle-aged man in a simple robe with a book and quarter staff shouted above everyone else, "Neskar, you have finally come to join the other prophets at our village! Come with us and bless us with your divine presence!"

Startled, Menkaure stopped and looked around to make sure that this stranger was talking about him. The man ran up close and bent to his knees, dropped the book and staff, clasped his hands in front of him and began to plead. Bloodshot green eyes looked up at Menkaure with unmistakable insanity. Long, black, matted hair and beard gave an idea as to how long his mind had been broken.

"Please, Neskar, come home with me to bring life back to my village and save us from certain death!"

Menkaure warily replied, "I am not this Neskar you speak of. You have me confused with someone else."

"No, no. You are Neskar! Look here!" Fumbling, the man picked up the book and opened it. Akhom rode up to the man and looked at the open page. He noticed that it seemed to be covered with stitched leather, and a closer look revealed the tattoo of an ancient priesthood.

"Look, look, it's you, Neskar." The man lifted the open book and pointed to a hand-drawn sketch that had an eerie resemblance. "Look, look!"

Menkaure took out a pair of brass-rimmed glasses, put them on and squinted at the sketch. "Oh my, that does look like me!" blurted Menkaure.

"Where do you come from?" Akhom asked the man, as he dismounted.

"I come from the northern plains. Our lands are sterile, my people starving. You must come with me and give us your blessings!" the man continued to plead. By this time a crowd had gathered to view the scene that was unfolding in front of them.

"I am sorry, but I can't go anywhere with you. I am needed elsewhere, far away from you!" Menkaure's horse, Merit, sensed panic in his voice and began to back away. The man dropped the book and got to his feet, all the while pleading, "You must. You must! I can't go back without you! I can't go back without you!" A look of rage came across the man's face as he drew a long dagger from the folds of his robe. "Then I will bring back only your head for the altar!" With that, the man stepped toward Menkaure. Instantly, and with a single word, Akhom channelled his defensive magic skills and focused it through his outstretched hand toward the attacker, stopping him in his tracks.

Akhom walked toward the paralysed man, still stuck in his attack pose. Concentrating on him, Akhom took off his left gauntlet and reached out to the man's temples. Unable to move, the man could only follow Akhom with his eyes. With a thumb and forefinger on either temple, Akhom spoke a command, "This is not the man you are looking for. Continue your search at the temple of Athena. Talk to the priests there and tell them that Akhom sent you. There you will find Neskar, but first you must sleep before your long journey. Akhom looked directly into his eyes and spoke the words, "Do as I command!"

The man crumpled to the ground, and said groggily, "Must get to temple. Must find Neskar. So tired, so tired." With that, the man fell into a deep sleep. Akhom dragged his limp body over to the fountain and propped him up, then took his book but left the staff. Turning to the crowd, he said, "No one is to bother this man! He must leave Nebetah when he wakes!" The crowd quickly moved away, amazed and frightened at such a powerful display of magic.

"Why did you command that mad man to go to your temple?" asked Menkaure.

"My brothers will help heal this man. The book has driven him mad. The ancient text in this book will possess anyone that reads it."

"How do you know that?" asked Menkaure.

"When I first saw the cover of the book it looked like patches of leather stitched together, but if you look closer there is a tattoo from an ancient, dead priesthood. They worshiped Hades."

"I have read only fragmented parchments that mention that name in passing," interjected Menkaure.

"Not surprising," responded Akhom. "His priests kept no written record except this book that Azmelqart commanded they make. Azmelqart was the first pontiff of the order, he told his acolytes that there were to be nine prophets, and apparently you are the ninth, or at least you look exactly like him. The cover of the book is human flesh taken from each prophet, and from the pontiff while he was still alive."

"How do you know all this, and why I am only just hearing it for the first time?" asked Menkaure.

"Simple," answered Akhom. "I am a priest of Athena; my brothers and I are encouraged to travel and learn. We seek out knowledge and you wait for knowledge to come to you."

"If this is the way you learn, then you can count me out," said Menkaure, with a slight laugh in his voice.

"I agree, let's not forget why we came here. We have food for the journey and now we have to find passage across the

Neferkare Sea." Akhom sniffed the wind and continued his thought. "The smell of rotting fish and the sea is strongest to the east. Let's go that way. And try not to be a prophet any more today!"

"You have my solemn word on that!" said Menkaure, with a wry smile.

Akhom mounted his horse and they set off for the docks.

The city streets became even more narrow and the buildings older as they got closer to the docks. The shipping district is where the first settlement took root at the shores of the Neferkare Sea. They asked people directions as they went, and soon found the harbourmaster's office. Outside the building, they stopped, and Menkaure said, "I don't think I will be of any use in there and I'm quite comfortable where I am." He petted Merit on the neck then added, "Besides, someone has to take care of the horses."

"OK, I'll agree to that." Akhom handed the reins over and walked toward the old mud brick building, it was buzzing with activity. As he walked in the main door, everyone stopped and noticed Akhom, completely out of place in the midst of the traders and ship captains looking for cargo to carry. Across the dimly lit room, Akhom saw a middle-aged man sitting behind a rickety old desk, flanked on either side by large men. Rather than talk to a captain directly, he knew to talk to the harbourmaster first and pay the fee. As Akhom approached the desk, the large men watched him closely and the crowd parted. The harbourmaster continued to write in his ledger. Akhom stopped in front of the desk and cleared his throat.

"Excuse me, sir, my friends and I seek passage to Dionysodoros."

The harbourmaster put down his stylus, held out his hand and said in a gravelly voice: "Three copper pieces."

Akhom paid the man. The harbourmaster flipped back a couple pages in his ledger, found the line with his finger and said, "Captain Ahinadab is laden with cargo but is heading that way. Talk to him, he might sell you passage on his ship." The harbourmaster pointed off into the left corner. Akhom turned and noticed a short, young, brown man in a red turban and matching robes stepping forward. The harbourmaster bent over his ledger with his pen and continued working.

Akhom walked across the room and stopped in front of Ahinadab.

"I'm at your service, mighty priest of Athena," he said, as he bowed with respect. With that, business continued as usual and the room filled with voices.

Akhom bowed as well, and said, "You can't be no more than eighteen."

"I will be seventeen this spring," Ahinadab said, with a smile. His small brown eyes were framed in a round face with a patchy beard.

"How can I be assured that such a young captain can get me and my friends across the Neferkare Sea unscathed?"

"I have lived on the sea all my life," answered Ahinadab. "My father inherited a cargo ship from his uncle. He met my mother on that ship, I was conceived on that ship and I was born on that ship. Now I have inherited that same ship and have sailed her across the three seas hundreds of times."

Akhom nodded to himself, and said, "How much for myself and three others? There are also three horses that are coming along."

"You said that there are four of you but only three horses?"

"The fourth member of our group is just too big for any horse to carry him," replied Akhom. "He walks wherever he goes. Come with me outside where it is a little quieter and you can meet my friend Menkaure."

On the way out of the building, Akhom asked, "How did you know I was a priest of Athena?"

"On my many voyages I was lucky enough to have one of your brethren aboard my ship for almost a year. All he wanted to do was travel and write in his journal. Also, his armour was green, just like yours, and when he wore his shield on his back, just as you are right now, he looked like a turtle," Ahinadab said, through a smile.

"That's right. We observe nature and try to learn from what comes natural, and the turtle is safe in its shell just like I am in my armour and shield. Did this other travelling turtle go by the name of Praxilaus?"

"Yes, yes!" Said Ahinadab, as he nodded his head.

"Praxilaus is the head of our order. My brethren and I strive to be the man he is."

They stopped in front of Menkaure and introductions were made. As they talked, Merit walked up to Ahinadab and gave him a good smell, finally concentrating on the pouch hanging from his waist. Merit gently pushed him with his head and neighed.

"Do you by chance have some dates in that pouch?" asked Menkaure.

"Yes, yes."

"She won't stop until she gets a couple of those sweet treats. I spoil her too much."

Ahinadab laughed and gave Merit some of his dates. As he fed Merit, he said, "My ship will be loaded with cargo by this evening but will not leave until the morning. Be at dock number six shortly after sunrise. I must warn you before you accept passage to Dionysodoros, there is a possibility that we will come across slaver ships, they know me and I carry their goods from time to time. It's no guarantee that they will leave you alone if they board and search my ship."

"From what I've heard, I think that you will be our best choice," answered Akhom. "We will be there without fail, but you still haven't told us the cost."

"When we get to Dionysodoros, then we can decide on that."

"Very well, then. We must be going if we want to make it back to camp before dark. One more thing," asked Akhom. "Where can we find a bottle of wine for our friend back at camp?"

"There is a shop beside the main gate of the city wall. You will find everything that you need there." Ahinadab pointed off to their left.

A man in the distance shouted for Ahinadab. He bowed quickly and was off to take care of business. Menkaure said, "He seems to be a trustworthy young man. I have a good feeling about him." Akhom got on his horse, then replied, "The Neferkare Sea is dangerous this time of year, bad storms…but I feel it too, that he will get us there alive," and with that, they went off to find Senusret a bottle of wine.

13

The rest of their time in Nebetah was uneventful. Akhom and Menkaure finished getting supplies for the journey across the sea and their long trek to Azerta. When they finally left the city, both of them felt a wave of relief. Nebetah could be a dangerous place. People from every corner of the three kingdoms and beyond pass through. When that many people are in close quarters, thieves are sure to be everywhere. Not only are fortunes stolen but lives as well. Bodies appear in the harbour almost every night. The ride to camp wasn't very far at all and both Akhom and Menkaure kept an eye open for anyone following. The sun began to set, but luckily Senusret and Gamden had a large fire burning that was easy to see from afar. As Akhom and Menkaure rode up, Senusret shouted out through a mouthful of food: "Hurry up! This deer is delicious and almost gone!"

Menkaure unraveled the ladder next to his saddle and climbed down saying, "You two managed to get a small deer for us tonight. That is amazing! How could you see it?"

Senusret was too busy eating, so Gamden answered for him.

"Kefu had a spyglass." He held it up for Menkaure to see. "We also found this bow that must be magical. When the arrow leaves the bow, it seems to disappear. We can never find the arrow. but it always finds its target."

"I will want to see both the spyglass and bow after we sup. That deer smells too good to wait."

Akhom asked Menkaure if he wanted Merit tied up with the other horses. "No, you don't have to worry about her. She won't leave my side." Menkaure petted her and gave her a date. Akhom took his horse over to Gamden's, took the saddles off both horses and gave them a quick brush.

"Akhom!" shouted Senusret. "Come eat or I will have to eat your share too!"

As he walked over to the fire, he took a look at his surroundings. They were in a small depression surrounded by large trees. He sat down and said, "I am sure that someone followed us from the city. I didn't see anything but I'm positive I heard footsteps following us."

Senusret stopped eating for a moment, looked around and said, "I'll go get 'em."

Akhom held up his hand and said, "I have a better idea. Where is Khepri?"

"He's around here somewhere. Khepri!" shouted Gamden. "Khepri!"

Everyone around the fire stopped what they were doing and looked for Khepri. Seconds later, he came out of the shadows and sat next to Gamden and got a pet for coming. "How does this work? I watched Kefu use his familiars before but never learned how."

"Remember back at the mansion when Kefu said that he was giving you his familiar?" answered Akhom. "Now you can command Khepri to do what you want. Get his attention, hold his head gently in your hand and look directly into his eyes. Tell him what to do and speak the word *irt* in the ancient tongue for "eye". You can use magic Gamden, he will do what you want."

Gamden did as Akhom told him. He took Khepri's head in his hand and said, "Go see who's out there Khepri, then come back." Gamden spoke the word. The shock of magical energy between the two startled them both. Khepri shook his head, meowed and leapt into the darkness.

"Now we wait." said Akhom. "He will find whoever is out there."

"How do I know when Khepri has found him?"

"When Khepri finds him, he will give you his sight," continued Akhom. "This is the first time you've done this. It will be disorienting at first, best to sit down the first few times or you will fall down. Senusret, you stay where you are, and I will sit on the other side of Gamden."

Akhom sat beside Gamden and their meal continued for only a few more minutes, when Gamden held up his hands and said, "I can't see the fire. Everything is black."

"Khepri has found his prey," said Akhom, with elation. "Tell us what you see and keep your voices quiet. He could be very near."

"Yes. Tell us what you see," whispered Menkaure. "I've never seen this done before. I'm scared to death, but so excited at the same time."

"I can see outlines now, but everything is grey. Too blurry to make out exact shapes." Gamden put his hands down and continued, "I can see clearer now."

"Concentrate!" whispered Akhom, in earnest. "You can do this."

"I wish that Khepri would get a little closer to him." No sooner had Gamden said it than he almost fell face-first into the fire. Senusret was quicker and sat him back up again. "I got so dizzy all of a sudden. My vision went blurry. Almost like I was moving but I didn't move at all."

"You can command Khepri while he shares his vision with you," cautioned Akhom. "In your mind tell him to slow down."

Gamden concentrated and said, "That's better, I don't feel so dizzy any more. I can see clear shapes now. He is walking around a large boulder."

"There is a boulder only thirty feet from here," whispered Menkaure, with fear.

Gamden said, "He is coming around the boulder now and I can see him. Only it's not a him, it's a girl. Looks pretty tiny but she has a small dagger."

Senusret laughed out loud and said, "Your first hunt and you bag a fawn instead of a buck!"

Everyone laughed, breaking the tension of the last few minutes. Gamden continued to describe what he saw: "Khepri is getting closer but the girl sees him now. She's running away!" Gamden concentrated, and commanded Khepri to stay where he was and watch her. "The girl has stopped and is hiding behind a bush. She looks to be more scared of us than anything. I'm going to have Khepri come back now, she's no threat." Khepri broke the link between them and came running back to the fire. Once back, he went straight to Gamden, sat in front of him and let out a loud meow.

Startled, Gamden said, "What do you want?" Khepri looked at the deer on the spit then back to Gamden. "Oh, that's what you want." Gamden got up, cut a piece off the deer and threw it to him. Khepri jumped in the air and caught it in his mouth, then settled down for a good meal, purring all the while.

"It would be a good idea if we kept watch through the night," warned Akhom. "This little girl could be a scout for a larger group waiting for an opportunity."

"That's a good idea," agreed Gamden. "I'll take first watch."

"Enough of all this useless talk," interjected Senusret. "It's a little girl. If I sat on her I would probably kill her. We'll be fine tonight. Now, where is that bottle of wine? I sure am thirsty, been a long day without a drop!"

"Merit, come here." She walked over to Menkaure. "Down," he said, and pointed to the ground. Merit slowly sat back on her haunches.

With a grunt, Menkaure got up and rummaged through the front saddlebag and pulled out a flagon of wine. "I got enough for everyone."

"Did you get a second for me?" asked Senusret.

"No, we can share it. There is enough for everyone. Besides, we have to save some for Gamden. He can't drink when he needs to stay up and watch the fire."

"I'm going to need more wine than that!" argued Senusret.

Menkaure waddled over to Akhom and handed him the flagon.

"Pour drinks for three, Akhom, while I get a pipe full of hashish ready for Senusret and me." With a smile, he dug in the saddlebag again.

Drinks were poured and handed out. Akhom remained standing, and said, "I offer this wine to Athena in tribute, so that she may grant us safe passage across the sea."

Senusret gulped his wine down while the other two sipped away at theirs. Menkaure cut off a large chunk of hashish from the block he brought with him and filled the pipe.

"OK, Senusret, this is going to knock you on your backside for the night. So you might as well find a comfortable place to sleep."

"Yeah, right," snorted Senusret, with derision. "I will be up all night with Gamden after that healing potion."

Menkaure clenched the bore of the pipe between his teeth while lighting a twig from the fire and said, "I grow the finest marijuana in all the three kingdoms and the hashish I make from it is a secret I keep for myself. If you are nice to me I just might make a little extra for you when we get back." Menkaure held the burning twig over the bowl of the pipe and inhaled slowly. With his lungs full, Menkaure sat back, smoke billowing out of his mouth and nostrils. Carefully, he waddled over to where Senusret was sitting, broke apart another chunk, placed it into the pipe and handed it over, saying, "Inhale slowly now, or you will cough all night long."

He took the pipe and the lit twig and did as he was told. Menkaure watched in amazement as all the hashish burned to ash. Senusret leaned back and exhaled enough smoke to envelop the campsite. "That tastes disgusting," he said, while making a sour face. "How can you smoke that all the time?" Slowly, Senusret's body visibly relaxed and he got himself very comfortable. "I'll have some more though, please," he said, as he lifted the pipe to be refilled. Everyone laughed, and the night went on.

"Now, Gamden, lets take a look at that spyglass and bow." Menkaure hobbled over and took the spyglass. Fishing out a magnifying glass hanging from around his neck, he looked carefully at the lens of the spyglass. "Ahh yes, just as I had thought. Kefu made this himself. If you look carefully you can see his crest inscribed. Such craftsmanship, the world lost a great man. I shall miss him." Menkaure stood silent for a moment, then came out of his reverie. "Sorry, sorry! Lost in my thoughts," he said, through a laugh.

"Lost in your hashish, more than anything!" said Akhom, jokingly. "You make your smoke too potent, old man. Just look at poor Senusret over there." He pointed to the big man sitting across the fire, squinty-eyed and smiling at nothing in particular.

"Yes, yes! Too potent!" laughed Menkaure. "I am just too old. Too old I say. The older I get the stronger my hashish gets and I'm very old indeed."

Changing the subject, Gamden asked, "What about the bow that we found in Kefu's basement?"

"Yes! Yes! Get me that bow, I need to see it," Menkaure answered, with excitement. Gamden reached behind him, produced the bow and handed it over. Menkaure ran his fingers from end to end of the upper and lower limbs. Not finding what he was looking for, he felt the tip then the recurve, where he found the runes. "I remember this now. Yes, I remember this. Kefu and I corresponded about this by courier pigeon. He said that a sudden storm came across his mansion and that lightning split an old oak tree in the back pasture."

Akhom interrupted by saying, "I remember that now, too. About five years ago when I stopped in to help him with his garden, Kefu had me knock down a tree that was split by lightning. While I was cutting it up he chose one branch in particular near the point where the bolt struck."

"Yes, yes." replied Menkaure, as he exhaled another lungful of smoke. "Kefu wrote that he had just made an offering of a goat to Zeus at his temple in Khaemwaset the day before. Taking it as a good omen, he asked me to write him back with runes in the ancient languages associated with Zeus."

"He obviously found the right combination of runes," answered Gamden. "I haven't found any of the arrows that I fired yet, every one was a kill shot."

Akhom, Menkaure and Gamden talked for a couple more hours; Senusret listened and laughed at almost everything they said while saying nothing himself. Soon, Senusret was snoring loudly, curled up by the fire to keep warm.

"That looks like a good idea," said Menkaure. "I am ready for sleep, too. Akhom, will you please clear away these stones and logs for me?"

"I'll help, too," said Gamden, and soon there was a clearing in front of the fire. Menkaure waddled over to the clearing and called Merit over to him. With expert skill, he used his walking stick to retrieve a large blanket and a bedroll from his saddle pack.

"Kneel down, girl," said Menkaure, as he pointed to the ground. Merit slowly got down on all fours beside him. In no time at all her saddle was off, and he had her lying on her side. The blanket was used to cover Merit's hindquarters and the bedroll between her legs made for a perfect cocoon. Not too much later, Akhom was sleeping comfortably as well, leaving Gamden to tend the fire for the first half of the night.

After reading several scrolls that he had taken from Kefu's mansion, Gamden's eyes became heavy and he dozed off a couple times. The third time he came out of a nap, the little girl from the outskirts of the camp was suddenly at the fire eating a handful of deer meat. "What do I do now?" he thought to himself. From across the fire he noticed that Akhom was watching her as well, through slit eyes. The girl was intent on eating as much as possible as fast as possible and didn't notice Akhom give a quick nod to Gamden, letting him know he was ready. Swiftly and silently, Akhom was up and moving toward the girl. She squealed in fear, spun around and started to run away. The trap was sprung and Gamden scooped her up in his arms. Kicking and screaming, the girl somehow got her arm free, and with knife in hand almost stabbed him, but Akhom was faster and took the dagger away.

"Who are you?" shouted Akhom.

"Let me go, asshole!" she shouted back, and then, with all her might, threw her head back into Gamden's chin. The girl went limp and Gamden slowly fell backward and hit the ground with a thud, girl still in his arms.

When the dust settled, Akhom stood there, noticing all was silent except for Senusret and Menkaure's loud snoring. He shook his head and said to himself, "I gotta try some of that hashish."

Minutes later, Gamden came to and saw the girl tied up across from him, still unconscious. He could taste the blood in his mouth from his split lip. "That's going to leave a mark," he said, as he slowly sat up."

"She hit you square in the mouth. Knocked you out cold," said Akhom, through a laugh.

"These two are still sleeping through all that noise. I gotta try some of that hashish," said Gamden, as he shook his head. "Did you find anything on her that could tell us who she is?"

"She is dressed in rags and reed sandals," Akhom said, as he pointed to the girl. "But it's this brand on her arm, she is a slave. I recognize it from one of the shops that Menkaure and I stopped at this afternoon when we were in the city. Most likely her master sent her out here to rob us in the night."

"Senusret will rip his head off if he comes across him in the city," replied Gamden. "Should we keep the girl here or take her back and set her free in the city?"

Akhom sat back and thought for a second, then said, "I think we should keep her here tonight. Tell Senusret about her in the morning, When we go to the docks we will have to pass by the shop, anyway. We have to remind him to keep his temper under control and we should be fine."

"Maybe you're right," said Gamden. "He won't be drunk, so he might listen to us."

The girl rolled onto her back, blinked twice then sat straight up with fear. "Who are you? What are you going to do to me?" she asked, as she struggled with her bonds.

Akhom held up his hands and said, "My name is Akhom. We don't want to hurt you. There is food and water next to you. I know you're hungry, so eat." She looked at both of them and then ate some of the deer meat. Akhom continued, "We have to go to the docks tomorrow. When we do, we will pass your master's shop."

"I have no master!" snapped the girl. "I ran away from that asshole! No one owns me!"

Gamden asked, "How old are you?"

"Fourteen," she said, pulling the matted long black hair away from her face. Missing teeth and dark circles under her eyes made it difficult to tell her age.

"You don't look any older than eight."

"Malnutrition from living on the streets," Akhom said. "What is your name?"

"My name is Oreithyia."

"When did you run away?"

"Don't know, long time ago," the girl said, through a mouthful of meat.

"How many winters since you ran away?"

The girl stopped chewing, thought about it for a couple of seconds and said, "Six winters."

"That means you were eight when you ran away," continued Gamden. "Do you know where your mother is?"

"I haven't seen her in a long time. She helped me run away. She said to go to the old temple guards and they would take me in. Bad men there so I run away again. Live with other kids in the sewers." Oreithyia took a big drink of water and said, "I hate sewers!"

Akhom looked at Gamden, then said, "We can't leave her alone here, she won't live for more than a couple more years."

Gamden shrugged his shoulders, and said, "You're right, we have to do something, but I don't know anyone around here and we have to board that ship tomorrow."

"I know what to do," said Akhom, with a smile. "When I traveled through Dionysodoros last time I met a sister of the Penthesilea convent. She will be well taken care of there. What do you think, Oreithyia?"

Curled up next to the fire fast asleep, she didn't say a thing.

"I guess we will find out in the morning," Akhom continued. "Why don't you get some sleep, too."

"I won't be sleeping any time soon," answered Gamden. "My lip is beating twice as fast as my heart. You get some rest and I will keep the fire going."

14

I n the morning after their campsite was cleaned up, everyone, including Oreithyia, made their way to the city. Before they got to the main gates, Gamden explained to Senusret what could happen if they pass the old shopkeeper on the way to the docks. "I won't do anything if he recognizes her," promised Senusret.

"OK, I'm trusting you not to draw attention to us," said Gamden. "We need to get to the docks on time."

Oreithyia rode with Akhom, she agreed to behave herself, so they cut her bindings. As they got closer to the city center, Oreithyia became visibly upset. Senusret walked beside her and tried to console her, with no results. Suddenly, from around the corner, the old shopkeeper appeared, flanked by four large men. Everything seemed fine as they passed each other on the street. From behind them, the old shopkeeper shouted, "Bodeshmun says you have my property!" At first, they ignored him and continued on their way. "If you don't give me the girl, my men will take her back!"

Senusret stopped dead in his tracks, and so did the group.

"Don't do it," whispered Gamden.

"I can't let her go back to that," he said, as he pointed to the old shopkeeper.

"Oh, you don't want to give her back!" said the disgusting old man. "Go get her, boys, and ten gold pieces to the one who can cut the balls off the big one!"

"Akhom, give me your shield."

"You can't use my shield if you intend to kill these men, Senusret."

"I won't kill them." Senusret held up his hand. "On my honour."

Akhom relented and handed over his shield. Dropping his weapon and Akhom's shield into his hand, Senusret charged into the fray. He smashed the first man in the face with the shield, and he dropped to the ground in a pool of blood. The second man fared no better, taking the shield square in the chest. It sent him flying through the air and he smashed against a brick wall.

"I didn't even break a sweat!" laughed Senusret.

The other two men looked at each other, nodded, and attacked simultaneously. Senusret parried a sword blow from the first man with his bracer and blocked the other man's spear with the shield, sending him stumbling off to the side.

Faster than either of the men could react, Senusret was on the offensive again. Blocking another sword thrust with the shield, Senusret kicked his opponent so hard he flew across the street into a cart full of fish.

"This is a joke!" laughed Senusret. "I thought we were going to fight."

Senusret walked towards the spearman, who tried to get away but Senusret was too fast. Throwing the shield, his aim was perfect and it struck the spearman in the back of the head. Senusret walked over and picked up the shield, then ran across the street to the cowering old shopkeeper. "Don't hurt me!" he said. "Take the girl! Just don't hurt me!"

With one arm, Senusret picked him up by his tunic, lifting him off the ground with ease. Looking the old shopkeeper in the eyes, Senusret said, "We will take the girl with us, and if I hear that you have abused any of your other slaves, I will come back here and rip out your diseased heart. I have friends everywhere in the city, watching you."

"I'll do whatever you say, just don't hurt me!" squealed the old shopkeeper.

Senusret put him down, and calmly said, "You're a disgusting old man, don't make me have to come back here."

The old shopkeeper ran away as fast as he could, with his henchmen close behind. Everyone on the street that had stopped to watch the fight broke out in cheers and threw garbage at the old man.

Senusret laughed out loud and walked back to his traveling mates. When he reached Akhom, he handed over the shield and said, "That was fun, I needed to get rid of my frustrations. Sorry about the blood." Senusret pointed to the crimson stain on the shield.

"That was impressive," said Akhom. "Where did you learn to fight like that?"

"I learned a little from my father but mostly from living on the streets," answered Senusret. "We better get going before that old man licks his wounds and comes back after me."

As they continued on their way to the docks, Oreithyia said, "Everyone hate old man. You first to beat him up. People like you now, I like you now too."

"I hate slavers too," said Senusret. "He was lucky that you were here, Akhom, or I would have left him hanging by the neck in front of his store."

"You sure have changed, Senusret. When we first met you would have killed them all," said Gamden. "I'm glad you can control your anger now."

"When we first met," replied Senusret, "I was ready to fight anyone for any reason. Now I can hardly find a reason to fight."

"Wiser words have never been spoken," said Menkaure.

The group turned the corner, and not too far away were the docks. The fresh sea air was a nice change from the smell of the city. When they finally made it to their destination, it was not too long until they found Ahinadab. Men were busy loading his ship with last-minute cargo.

"When the ship is loaded," said Ahinadab, "we will get your horses below deck. I had my men set up a stable for the trip. Unfortunately, space is limited on the ship and I have a full crew, you will be most comfortable with the horses. My men put down extra hay for you to sleep on." Ahinadab pulled a piece of straw from his turban. "It's comfortable, I can assure you. I also see that you have an extra passenger.

"My name is Oreithyia," she said, with a shy smile.

"Good to meet you, Oreithyia, my name is Ahinadab," he said with a bow and a big smile.

"Wait!" shouted Gamden. "Where is Khepri? Khepri!" he shouted again. With a loud meow Khepri stuck his head out of the saddlebag on Menkaure's horse.

Shortly after the last of the cargo was loaded, the horses were led to the stable and the ship was ready to sail. The mooring was released and six men with long, thick, wooden polls pushed the ship safely away from the dock. The crew jumped into action getting the ship ready to be put to sea. The sails caught the wind and the ship lurched forward. Their course was set for Dionysodoros and then Azerta. There was no going back now.

15

The first day of the voyage saw them make good speed across smooth waters. There wasn't too much to do, Ahinadab and his crew kept a clean vessel. Gamden couldn't complain about this crossing, even though he hated travelling over water. Oreithyia watched Ahinadab from afar and was coy when near him, but did her best to stay close. That night, one of the crewmen caught a large fish and roasted it over a brazier. With their bellies full, everyone slept contentedly.

The next morning saw clear skies but no wind, and their progress stalled. Ahinadab had no love for this, he knew that at this time of year the winter season brought storms. Ships loaded to capacity sink fast and leave no survivors. The morning was almost done when the clouds rolled in from the west, and with them came the rain. Ahinadab ordered full sail in the growing wind to outrun the storm brewing behind them. The first of the waves started to rock the ship soon thereafter and the captain ordered half sail. Four men manned the rudder at all times, trying their best to keep the craft on course.

Down below decks, Gamden and everyone else were being tossed about as each wave crashed into the ship. The horses were growing restless, neighing loudly as they smashed into the walls of their stable.

Gamden complained, "I hate this shit! Every time I get on a boat there is a storm or something that's going to kill me!"

"I have crossed the Neferkare Sea many times," said Akhom. "Through storms worse than this and I made it every time, and we will survive this storm too."

Seconds later, the hatch burst open above then, rain and cold wind poured into the lower decks. Three men came stumbling down the stairs, shouting, "The rudder broke loose, it struck Amytis in the chest! I think his ribs are broken, help him!" The two men laid the third in the hay, then one ran back up the stairs to close the hatch.

Everyone was up and ready to help. Menkaure said, "Akhom, your brotherhood practice healing magic. Can you help him?"

"I think I can," said Akhom, as he moved to aid the man. "Take his jacket and undershirt off. Gently!" Slowly the two men did as he said, and once his shirt was off they could see a dark blue bruise stretched across his chest, a perfect outline of where the rudder hit him, every breath a fight to live just a little longer.

Akhom raised his hands palms up to the sky and said, "Athena hear me and give your strength to help this wounded man." He then touched his left middle finger and forefinger to his lips, then his forehead. He spoke the ancient word for heal: "Iaomai."

Laying his hands on the wounded man's chest, a bright green glow came over his whole body as the healing magic of Athena discharged from him.

The man relaxed and took several deep breaths, then slowly opened his eyes. "What happened? he asked. "Where am I?"

Everyone waited for Akhom to answer him, but when he took his hands off the man he fell backwards into Senusret's arms.

"Amytis, my brother, you're alive. We thought the gods had taken you from us!"

"I'm alive, thanks be to Athena," said Amytis. "Tell me, brother, where is the priest that saved me, I must thank him!"

"Using that much magic at once," answered Menkaure, "has drained all his strength. He must sleep now, pray to Athena that he may recover quickly."

"We will pray and make offerings unto her for many weeks to come." The three men bowed deeply, then rushed up the stairs and out onto the deck to battle the storm again.

Gamden closed the hatch, then said as he kneeled down beside Akhom, "I have never seen that kind of magic used before. Sure, I've seen simple healing spells used before for small wounds, but that was something completely different."

"Akhom has devoted his entire life to Athena," responded Menkaure. "He has learned to use the magic given to his brotherhood, it's a potent magic and it can exact a potent price."

"How long will he have to rest?" asked Gamden.

"Difficult to tell. Could be as short as a couple hours or maybe through the night."

"Well, it's going to be a long night," said Senusret. "Why don't you break off another chunk of that hashish and we'll settle in for the long haul.

16

The storm bashed and battered the ship for the rest of the night. The crew took shifts manning the rudder and Captain Ahinadab was with them every minute of the struggle. Shortly after sunrise, the storm began to break and calm seas returned. Exhausted, the captain ordered full sails again, then went to his cabin and fell into a deep sleep.

Gamden, Senusret and Menkaure ventured out onto the deck. After spending the night cooped up in a stable, the fresh air was delicious. Oreithyia was quick on their heels and asked, "Where Ahinadab?"

One of the deckhands shouted out, "He went to his cabin to sleep, he could barely stand up anymore."

"I take him food, I take care of him," Oreithyia left to get food and water to take to the captain's quarters. Shortly after that, Akhom made his way up the stairs into the sunlight and fresh sea breeze. Gamden was the first to see him and asked,

"How do you feel? You look a lot better, you were white as a ghost last night."

"I do feel better this morning," said Akhom, as he rubbed his eyes in the bright sunlight.

Gamden walked over to him, grabbed him by the shoulder and said, "How did you save him? He was ready to join his family in Elysium."

"Athena chooses when to give me and my brothers all her power. When we save the lives of the innocent she is pleased, and her magic is strong." Akhom stopped talking and stretched, then continued, "I'm starving, I haven't eaten since yesterday. What do we have to eat?"

"Yeah! When are we going to eat!" shouted Senusret. The crewmen close by heard and shouted, "Akhom is hungry! Akhom is hungry!" He then ran away and came back with his arms overflowing with food and drink for the party. He handed the food over and thanked both of them several times, then bowed deeply.

"Thank you for the food," said Akhom, "but I'm very hungry and I'm sure that Senusret can eat twice as much as me."

"You bet I can!" answered Senusret, as he bit into a giant apple. The man ran off to get more people and more food.

Both Akhom and Senusret ate until they were stuffed, then found comfortable spots to lay down in the sun and fell asleep.

The rest of the afternoon was uneventful, and they made good speed with a strong wind. Ahinadab was walking across the deck with Oreithyia close by him. He made his way to where Gamden and Menkaure were standing and said, "Amytis owes his life to Akhom. If he weren't here, I would be mourning the loss of a crewmate. It's a good omen."

"Where is Amytis?" asked Gamden.

"After Amytis came back from being healed by Akhom, he said that he had the strength of three men. He took the rudder from us and steered the ship through the storm. When the storm was over he was so exhausted that he collapsed. He's still sleeping now."

"Athena's magic affects everyone in different ways," said Menkaure. "She protects those who are in danger and she can also give strength to those that need it."

"That's right," said Akhom, as he walked up into the conversation.

"I've never tried to heal a person with those kinds of injuries before. My teacher, Praxilaus, once healed a man on the battlefield that should have died. Not only was he healed, but Athena's magic gave him super-human strength. He got up, ran back into the melee and won the day."

Gamden said in amazement, "Is Praxilaus a warrior priest like you?"

"No, he is a healer only. He will not harm a person in any way."

"Kefu told me," continued Gamden, "that humans are able to use magic because of creatures like dragons, wyverns and minotaurs, but how can a priest use magic?"

"Priests and a select few clergy can use magic because we are chosen by our gods to do his or her bidding. Through Athena I can heal and defend. Menkaure worships Hermes, so he and his brothers are the scribes of the gods. He uses divination to unlock codes, spells and languages; he can see future events and find hidden things or people."

"But mages like Kefu, and you too, Gamden.," interjected Menkaure, "channel the magical energy that creatures like dragons and those all the way down to the lowly cerastes emanate. When all the dragons and their kind are gone, magic will disappear with them."

"Why, then," Gamden asked, with a puzzled look on his face, "do mages have to use magical words and phrases? I mean, can't they just think it and it happens?"

"As I said," answered Menkaure, "humans channel magic, we are not inherently magic. No. Not at all. Not at all! Magical words and phrases give substance to the magic. Allows it to take a physical form in our world."

Gamden shook his head in confusion, and said, "I just don't understand. How can I use something if I don't know what it is or where it comes from?"

With his eyes closed and in a calm voice, Akhom said, "Do not question why the gods have chosen you for magic. They have reasons that we can never understand. It is a gift to you, use it to do good in this world and you will be rewarded with eternal life in Elysium. Praise be to Athena." He touched his left middle finger and forefinger to his lips, then his forehead.

High atop the main mast, a crewman shouted from the crow's nest: "Captain! Captain! A ship on the horizon."

Ahinadab shouted back, "What flag is she flying?"

The man in the crow's nest looked again through his spyglass and answered, "Blue and black with a white crescent moon!"

"Damn!" said Ahinadab, with a look of worry on his face. "I have never traded with these slavers before and they are not looking to do so now. This is very dangerous. Slaver ships are small and fast. They'll catch us long before we get to Dionysodoros, and we're already at full sail."

"When will the slaver ship overtake us?" asked Menkaure.

Ahinadab thought about it for a moment. "I think they'll catch us in…eight hours, maybe nine."

"That would put us in the early morning before sunrise?"

"Yes, just before sunrise," answered Ahinadab.

"Why don't we do this," continued Menkaure. "Let them get almost within range of using grappling hooks and then, when they think they've got us, Gamden can cast a powerful sleep spell."

Gamden looked at Menkaure dumbfounded, and asked, "And how will I do that, with a lullaby?"

"No!" said Menkaure, with a laugh. "With the spell I memorised when I visited Kefu many years ago. It will put everyone on that ship to sleep where they stand."

"I'll try, but I've never used that kind of magic before."

"No need to worry," Menkaure reassured Gamden. "Works every time!"

Day turned to night and everyone was on edge. Menkaure prepared Gamden as best he could for the trap they were going to spring. Ahinadab tried his best to lose the other ship in the dark, changing course many times. During the fourth course change, when Menkaure was ready to lay down for a sleep, he suddenly sat up and yelled out in pain.

"What's wrong?" asked Gamden. "Are you hurt!"

"Someone on that slaver ship is using a divination spell to find where we are," said Menkaure, as he pressed his fingers against his temples. "I need to break their spell." He pressed his palms together, fingers up, and touched them to his forehead. Chanting in a long-dead language, he concentrated on breaking the spell. After what seemed like an eternity, Menkaure relaxed with a sigh of relief.

"What happened?" asked Gamden. "Did you break the spell? Did they find us?"

"I was able to break the spell," replied Menkaure. "And I left them with a nasty surprise. Their witch will be unconscious for a couple days." He laid back into the bale of hay and continued with a smile, "I hate witches. Devious and powerful, the lot of them."

With the skill of Ahinadab at the rudder and the breaking of the witch's spell, they managed to throw the slaver ship off their trail. Shortly after sunrise, the slavers located them and the chase was on again. The slaver ship made good speed through the night and the gap between the ships quickly disappeared. The hatch to the stable flew open and a crewman shouted, "Prepare to be boarded! Ship in sight!" The party got to their feet and went above deck into the growing daylight.

"Now, Gamden," said Menkaure. "We need to wait until the slaver ship is almost ready to throw grappling hooks, then you drink the potion and recite the phrase of Phobetor. Then face the slaver ship and shout out the trigger word."

"Phrase of Phobetor. Trigger word," repeated Gamden, while he nodded.

"Well, recite the words then, until you have it perfect!" goaded Menkaure.

Gamden repeated the words perfectly three times for his teacher. "I'm impressed!" laughed Senusret. "Not bad for a second-rate thief."

"Senusret, don't say that!" scolded Akhom. "At best, third rate, truth be told!"

Everyone laughed, breaking the tension of the moment. Within that short time span, the slaver ship closed the gap, and stray arrows started landing on the deck and in the sails.

Menkaure gathered up Ahinadab, told him to get most of his men below deck except for what he needed to keep the ship sailing. "If any of us hears the trigger word, we will all fall into a sleep filled with nightmares." The deck was cleared quickly. Akhom cast a spell to protect himself, Menkaure and Senusret from Gamden's magic. The rudder was tied off and everyone else hid from sight, waiting for the moment to spring their surprise.

Shouts from the slaver ship could be heard, and one of their sails was furled. Slowly, they came alongside, slavers ready to board.

"Now!" shouted Menkaure.

Gamden swallowed the potion in one gulp, trying his best not to vomit from the poisonous concoction. He stood up with a feeling of absolute clarity of thought, held his hands out front of him and, with the voice of a titan, he spoke the phrase of Phobetor. His words compelled the slavers to look directly at him. . Then the trigger word: "Oneiri." The word boomed out of Gamden's chest, summoning the power of the god of nightmares. The people on the slaver ship fell to the deck in a deep sleep filled with the most gruesome nightmares. With no one at the rudder, the slaver ship veered toward them, almost crashing into their ship. Men from below decks ran up top to get control of the rudder. When they saw all their crewmates laying as if dead all around them, the slavers made every effort to get away.

Gamden shouted in triumph and turned to his friends. "I did it! I never did anything like that before, but I did it!" His knees almost buckled, and he reached for the ship's rail. "I feel like someone hit me over the head. Is it always like this, potions I mean?"

"This is the first time you've used a potion," said Akhom. "By using them more you'll become accustomed to their effects. Just like Senusret and how he can drink so much wine."

"Hey!" replied Senusret, with a frown. "No need to rub it in!"

"I meant it as a compliment," said Akhom. "Every mage or priest has their own limit, of course. Some potions can be quite poisonous and could kill you if you use them too often."

"I don't like this at all." Gamden's head rolled back and he fought off the urge to vomit.

"You'll be OK in a couple of hours," said Menkaure, with reassuring smile.

The rest of the day brought no more trouble and they made good speed with a robust wind in the sails. They were leaving the lawless part of the sea and entering the protected waters of Dionysodoros. Heavy warships patrolled, keeping the slavers at bay.

On the last day of the voyage, far off in the distance along the eastern border, Mount Phaethusa was belching fire and smoke. That meant they were close, and every minute brought them closer to their destination. The tensions of the crew melted away. The day was warm and sunny by the time they reached the harbour walls. Several warships were anchored nearby, reminding all that King Cyaxares was firmly in control and ready to take back the eastern wildlands.

When they were finally able to dock, everyone on board was ready to get their feet on dry land.

17

After everyone, including the horses, were safely on the dock, Ahinadab found Gamden and the rest of the party. "Where are you off to now?" asked Ahinadab. He had changed the colour of the turban he wore to green so that he fit in with the local merchants. "With all those supplies you must be going to the end of the Earth."

"No, nothing like that at all. Just visiting friends," answered Gamden.

"Yes…of course. Visiting friends," said Ahinadab, through a smile. "We'll leave it at that."

Changing the subject quickly, Gamden asked, "How much for bringing us to Dionysodoros?"

"You owe me nothing," said Ahinadab, with a wave of his hand. "A priest of Athena is always welcome to travel on my ship whenever he wishes."

"That is very generous of you," answered Akhom, with a shallow bow.

"Maybe when you get back from visiting your friends you will sail with me again."

"After that crossing I think I'll walk back home," Gamden said, with a smile. "Every time I set foot on a ship a storm or something else seems to want me dead."

"You always seem to make it out alive, though," joked Senusret. "You always come walking back into my life when I least expect it."

"The best gifts," interjected Menkaure, "are always appreciated most when they come unexpectedly."

"And I am such a great gift," said Gamden, through a grin.

When everyone finished laughing, Senusret asked, "Ahinadab, where is Oreithyia, we best be going soon. Get her to Penthesilea convent and then something into my belly. I'm starving!"

"Actually, Oreithyia has decided to stay with me." Ahinadab pointed up to the bow of the ship where she stood surrounded by women from the local shops who were fussing over her hair and clothes. She looked directly at Senusret and mouthed the words "thank you," while holding her hands over her heart.

"When you see her next time, she will be my bride."

Everyone shouted their congratulations to Ahinadab, and when the last of the handshakes were over, the party mounted their horses.

"Wait, where is Khepri?" asked Gamden with concern, as he looked around. From behind them came a loud meow, and he came running at full speed and leapt up into Gamden's lap with a fish in his mouth.

"Hey, you!" a local merchant shouted at Gamden. "Your cat just stole that fish right off my cart!"

"Sorry about that," said Gamden, through a laugh. "My cat is just like my friend here." As he pointed to Senusret, he continued, "They both think with their stomachs. I hope this will cover the cost." Gamden tossed him a silver coin.

"Are you kidding me?" The merchant said, with disdain. "That fish is worth twice as much!"

Gamden knew that was an outrageous lie and said, "Senusret, why don't you explain to the nice man that a silver coin will do just fine."

Senusret walked across the lane, towered over the merchant and said in a menacing tone: "My friend is being very generous in giving you a silver piece. Take it and be happy!"

The merchant cowered and said in a feeble voice: "Yes… yes I'm very happy. Thank you…thank you," then ran back to his cart.

Menkaure said, "We better get going. We've been here less than an hour and already an altercation. The sooner we get out of this city the better."

"I agree," interjected Akhom. "But first we need to stop at Penthesilea convent and get the blessing of the sacred mother.

All that travel into the eastern wild lands will require it, or ill fortune will beset us."

Everyone in the group agreed that it would be best to do so and started off to the convent. In the distance, they could see where they needed to go. The convent was the original fortress of the city. Many generations ago, the first sacred mother and sisters took over the citadel and turned it into a sanctuary of peace. Dionysodoros has been razed and rebuilt many times, but always the convent stood.

Armed guards patrol the city continuously, watching for radical eastern wildmen attacking without warning and killing innocent people, then disappearing into the crowded streets. King Cyaxares rules with an idea of retaking the old eastern realms through diplomacy, but also with an understanding that force will be needed too. When the city was last retaken from the wildmen, the King knew that he couldn't rein in all the eastern peoples. Instead of persecution, he chose assimilation of the eastern cultures. For the most part, the King's subjects and the eastern people live together in peace. The eastern royal families beyond Azerta ally themselves with the cyclops, arm and feed his soldiers while keeping his coffers overflowing with gold. In return, the cyclops gets to stay in Azerta as long as he maintains a constant state of siege on Dionysodoros. Conversely, the three western kingdoms fund the majority of King Cyaxares' efforts in Dionysodoros.

The party made their way through the streets toward the convent. Most of the buildings were still leveled but new structures were being built. Heaps of rubble made the roads clogged and slow-moving. The rubble that wasn't being taken away was used for new houses and businesses. The massive rebuilding projects in the city meant that the King was ready to spread his wealth around. When the people and tradesmen were busy working, everyone was happy and King Cyaxares was more popular than ever before.

"How old is this city?" asked Gamden.

Menkaure answered him with: "Dionysodoros is the first attempt of the western peoples to conquer the eastern plains. Only scattered settlements were found, and little resistance was offered from the people. When the western armies made it to Azerta, stiff resistance was coming from the eastern royal families and the decision was made to build the fortress."

"That really doesn't answer my question, though," said Gamden, through a laugh.

"Sorry! I tend to ramble then go way off subject." After his apology, Menkaure continued, "The ancient scrolls at Amunet monastery tell of a hundred generations of men that have lived, fought and died in Dionysodoros. The city has fallen three times to the eastern wildmen and every time we retake it the people have to live in a constant state of siege."

"May Athena grant us all peace and health," said Akhom, with his palms to the sky. All the while his horse slowly made its way down the street.

"Peace and health," repeated Menkaure, then continued, "But I have seen plans for something that will allow us to hold the city and maybe even take back Azerta from the cyclops monarch."

After a short pause, Gamden couldn't handle the wait any longer and shouted, "Well, what is it then? Don't keep us in suspense!"

Menkaure looked at him with a sly grin and said, "Ballistics."

The conversation turned a little too in-depth for Senusret, and his head was spinning from all the terms he had never heard before. Senusret stopped dead in his tracks, shook his head and said in a frustrated voice, "I have no idea what you guys are talking about, say it in words I can understand!"

"Sorry, buddy. Didn't mean to do that," Gamden said to Senusret. Then he thought about how could explain it to him so that he could understand. "A-ha! I know, hold on a moment." He rummaged through the saddle pack and took out the grenade they found in Kefu's mansion. "Remember how I said this was full of explosives?"

"Yeah…yeah, I remember that," nodded Senusret. "Boom!"

"That's right," continued Gamden. "Right now, it will only go as far as I can throw it, but with ballistics it can go as far the other side of the city."

Senusret turned away and squinted off into the distance, then turned back and said, "I can barely see that far away, but we wouldn't need it. I think I could still throw it that far."

Everyone laughed and continued down the street to the convent.

Even off in the distance the convent could be seen. Its tall stone walls towered over the surrounding buildings. Throughout the years that the old fort has stood, no army has tried to occupy it. The sacred sisters provided healing and food to those who needed it, whether friend or foe. When they finally reached their destination, the main gates were wide open and there wasn't a soldier in sight. The inner courtyard was immaculate, the trees were in full bloom and a scent of freshly-trimmed hedges filled their nostrils. Everyone who entered the convent immediately felt at peace. As the party made their way up the stairs to the inner sanctum, one of the sisters came out in her turquoise robes and greeted them.

"Hello, weary travelers, I see that you bear arms. Are your intentions virtuous or villainous?"

Akhom stepped forward and returned the greeting. "Sacred sister, my name is Akhom, Priest of Athena. These are my traveling companions. We are going into the eastern wildlands. We seek the Sacred Mother's blessing for safe travels."

"A priest of Athena!" the sister exclaimed. "We are truly blessed to have you in our home, and welcome to your friends as well."

"Is Belit available to see visitors?"

"No, Master Akhom," replied the sister. "She is asleep in her quarters. She was up all night tending to the sick that came in last night. Terrible sickness in the city."

"Maybe when we come back through Dionysodoros we will stop in again."

"We look forward to it!" said the sister, with a smile. "Now, come with me and I will take you to the Sacred Mother." With a flutter of her turquoise robe, she spun around and led the way.

"What will we do with the horses?" asked Gamden.

"The grass is green and deep," answered Menkaure. "They will graze until we get back. Besides, Merit will keep an eye on them, won't you, girl?" He gave her a pat on the nose and the horses walked off into the grass to enjoy themselves.

The inside of the old fortress starkly contrasted to the outside. The outer walls were plain stone, but the inside was painted in white and turquoise. The floors had ornate tile work, and frescos decorated many hallways. They finally came into the hall where the Sacred Mother was relaxing on the old King's throne. She presented as an odd sight to behold. A shriveled old woman sitting in a giant chair, feet dangling in the air. Gamden was the last of the party to enter, and as he did the Sacred Mother shrieked in pain. Several sisters came running to her side. "What is the matter?!" they asked.

"The light, it hurts my eyes! It burns my eyes and there is a fire in my mind!" She seemed to shrink even further back into the chair.

"Sacred Mother, you are blind, you have been for many years." The sisters asked: "How can you see us now?"

"I only see him!" she croaked, and pointed directly at Gamden. "He has an aura of blinding white light!"

"Do you want him to leave, Sacred Mother?"

"No! No, he doesn't have to leave, the light is becoming more bearable. Come to me, I want to see you up close." The Sacred Mother gestured for Gamden to come closer. Gamden was reluctant as first, but relented and slowly made his way to the throne chair. Sacred Mother stood up and straightened her turquoise robes, then removed her headdress. Doing so revealed a wrinkled face like the trunk of a tree and eyes that were completely clouded over with cataracts.

"Come closer, young one." Gamden resisted the urge to come closer but the Sacred Mother gestured to him, and he found himself walking toward her. When he was literally nose-to-nose with the Sacred Mother, she took his head in her hands, turned his head this way and that, then looked into his eyes. Not finding what she wanted, the Sacred Mother held the back of his head with one hand and placed the palm of the other against his forehead and closed her eyes. A look of total concentration came across her face, which then turned to a grimace of pain. When the pain became unbearable, the Sacred Mother released her grip on Gamden and fell back into her chair. Gamden stumbled for a moment then regained his balance.

"What just happened?" asked Gamden. "I remember looking into her eyes, then she was in the chair!"

Menkaure walked up to his side and said, "The Sacred Mother looked into your mind. Into your *mind*." He emphasised by tapping the temple of his own forehead. "Whatever she saw was too much for her to take all at once. She is a powerful seer, whatever is going on in that head of yours stopped her dead in her tracks."

"But I…but I don't even know what I did," stammered Gamden.

"Silence!" commanded the Sacred mother. "I'm tired and my head hurts. I must lay down."

Whispered voices from the sisters erupted, "Sacred Mother hasn't spoken in weeks. Sacred Mother stood up. Sacred Mother sees again."

"No, Sacred Mother can't see again!" she said of herself to the sisters, in a mocking tone. "And I haven't had anything interesting to stay. I'm a hundred and eight years old, I've run out of interesting things to say! You four get out of here too, especially the young one. You are the reason my head hurts."

"Sacred Mother!" interrupted Akhom. "We need your blessing for safe travels into the wildlands!"

"You don't need my protection from your enemies," answered Sacred Mother, as she pointed to Gamden with a bony finger.

"Your enemies will need protection from him!"

From behind the chair came a tall woman who scooped up the Sacred Mother in her arms like a rag doll. In a flurry of turquoise robes, the sisters left the room and the party stood dumbfounded. Breaking the silence, Senusret said, "I guess that we should see ourselves out, then." They all looked at each other and turned to leave.

They gathered up the horses and were ready to make their way out of the city, when one of the sisters came running across the courtyard to them. "Sacred Mother wants you to know that she is feeling better now and that she will pray for your safe passage through the wildlands."

A look of relief came over Akhom's face as he heard the news.

"Also, Master Gamden, Sacred Mother wants you to come back and see her when you return from Azerta."

With a stunned look on his face, Gamden said, "How did she know that we are going to Azerta?"

"Remember what I told you," said Menkaure. "She is a seer, she read your thoughts. No one can hide their thoughts from the Sacred Mother when she wants the truth."

The sister bowed and wished them safe travels, then turned and ran up the stairs into the convent. "I don't understand why all of this is happening now," said Gamden. "Everything is changing so fast. First Kefu is dead and then Menkaure said that he came to him in a dream and talked about miraculous events. Now the Sacred Mother...I just don't understand!"

Menkaure took Gamden's hand, motioned for him to get on one knee so he could look him in the eye and said, "Sometimes life changes fast and it's difficult to make sense of it all. We've got to go forward and see what's going to happen, good or bad."

"I'll be honest," said Gamden. "I'm scared out of my wits. But you're right, we have to go on, good or bad."

"Hey, no need to worry!" interrupted Senusret, as he got down on one knee beside them. "You got us to watch your back." He gave Gamden a punch to the shoulder.

Rubbing his shoulder, Gamden said with a smile, "Thanks, ya big bastard."

The party mounted their steeds and made their way out of the convent. The mood was somber as they slowly traversed the crowded streets. Senusret, as usual, complained that they never stopped at any taverns when he was thirsty or hungry. Everyone reminded him that he was always thirsty. After a couple of wrong turns, they found the proper route through the city until the main gates stood before them. In the distance, rolling hills stretched out before them, covered in a dense forest.

"We have at least a month's hard travel there and back," said Akhom. "Do we have everything and everyone?" Gamden checked his saddlebag, found Khepri sleeping soundly and gave a thumbs-up.

"Wait!" blurted out Senusret. "We need more wine!"

Akhom reached into his shoulder bag and pulled out an apple.

"Here," he said, and tossed him the apple. "Chew on this, keep your mouth busy."

Senusret caught it and took a big bite. "Mmm, delicious," he said, through a mouthful.

"Let's get going," said Gamden through a laugh, and he led the way.

The main road was busy, and they had to travel off to the side of it. Three rickety covered wagons passed them with two men each on the front bench seat. Only a few seconds later, one man from each wagon jumped down and ran to the back of the wagons. Tearing away the tarps revealed large kegs filled with explosives. Fuses were lit, whips cracked, and the horses charged the main gate. Screams erupted from the innocent people jumping out of the way of the wagons. As the party turned to see what was happening, horns blasted from the guard towers warning of the impending danger. Orders were shouted and the thick ropes holding the counterweights for the main gate were cut, dropping it down with an ear-shattering clang.

The wagons kept on going at full speed, the horses frothing at the mouth with exertion. With no time for the guards to react, the wagons piled into the main gates; a split second later the explosives detonated, deafening the party and spooking the horses. Senusret was fast and grabbed the reigns of all three horses, stopping them from bolting. To their left and right, armed men came charging out of the forest, anticipating the main gate being blown to pieces. Guards in the gate towers rained down arrows on the attacking force.

Menkaure shouted over the clamour and the ringing in their ears: "What have we gotten ourselves into?"

Akhom shouted back, "The cyclops mercenaries are attacking again. Let's get going so we don't get caught up in this."

He took his horse's reigns from Senusret, spurred his horse and set off for the forest. As the rest of the party followed, Gamden looked back, and when he saw the convent in the distance he remembered the words of the Sacred Mother: "You will not need protection from your enemies. Your enemies will need protection from him."

Lightning Source UK Ltd.
Milton Keynes UK
UKHW01f1307200718
326035UK00006B/854/P